Acting Edition

Natasha, Pierre & The Great Comet of 1812

by Dave Malloy

Adapted from *War and Peace*
by Leo Tolstoy

‖SAMUEL FRENCH‖

Copyright © © 2013, 2014, 2017 by Dave Malloy
Foreward Copyright © 2014, 2017 by Rachel Chavkin
All Rights Reserved
Second Edition

NATASHA, PIERRE & THE GREAT COMET OF 1812 is fully protected under the copyright laws of the United States of America, the British Commonwealth, including Canada, and all member countries of the Berne Convention for the Protection of Literary and Artistic Works, the Universal Copyright Convention, and/or the World Trade Organization conforming to the Agreement on Trade Related Aspects of Intellectual Property Rights. All rights, including professional and amateur stage productions, recitation, lecturing, public reading, motion picture, radio broadcasting, television, online/digital production, and the rights of translation into foreign languages are strictly reserved.

ISBN978-0-573-70283-9

www.concordtheatricals.com
www.concordtheatricals.co.uk

FOR PRODUCTION INQUIRIES

UNITED STATES AND CANADA
info@concordtheatricals.com
1-866-979-0447

UNITED KINGDOM AND EUROPE
licensing@concordtheatricals.co.uk
020-7054-7200

Each title is subject to availability from Concord Theatricals Corp., depending upon country of performance. Please be aware that *NATASHA, PIERRE & THE GREAT COMET OF 1812* may not be licensed by Concord Theatricals Corp. in your territory. Professional and amateur producers should contact the nearest Concord Theatricals Corp. office or licensing partner to verify availability.

CAUTION: Professional and amateur producers are hereby warned that *NATASHA, PIERRE & THE GREAT COMET OF 1812* is subject to a licensing fee. The purchase, renting, lending or use of this book does not constitute a license to perform this title(s), which license must be obtained from Concord Theatricals Corp. prior to any performance. Performance of this title(s) without a license is a violation of federal law and may subject the producer and/or presenter of such performances to civil penalties. Both amateurs and professionals considering a production are strongly advised to apply to the appropriate agent before starting rehearsals, advertising, or booking a theatre. A licensing fee must be paid whether the title(s) is presented for charity or gain and whether or not admission is charged. Professional/Stock licensing fees are quoted upon application to Concord Theatricals Corp.

This work is published by Samuel French, an imprint of Concord Theatricals Corp.

No one shall make any changes in this title(s) for the purpose of production. No part of this book may be reproduced, stored in a retrieval system, scanned, uploaded, or transmitted in any form, by any means, now known or yet to be invented, including mechanical, electronic, digital, photocopying, recording, videotaping, or otherwise, without the prior written permission of the publisher. No one shall share this title(s), or any part of this title(s), through any social media or file hosting websites.

For all inquiries regarding motion picture, television, online/digital and other media rights, please contact Concord Theatricals Corp.

MUSIC AND THIRD-PARTY MATERIALS USE NOTE

Licensees are solely responsible for obtaining formal written permission from copyright owners to use copyrighted music and/or other copyrighted third-party materials (e.g., artworks, logos) in the performance of this play and are strongly cautioned to do so. If no such permission is obtained by the licensee, then the licensee must use only original music and materials that the licensee owns and controls. Licensees are solely responsible and liable for clearances of all third-party copyrighted materials, including without limitation music, and shall indemnify the copyright owners of the play(s) and their licensing agent, Concord Theatricals Corp., against any costs, expenses, losses and liabilities arising from the use of such copyrighted third-party materials by licensees. For music, please contact the appropriate music licensing authority in your territory for the rights to any incidental music.

IMPORTANT BILLING AND CREDIT REQUIREMENTS

If you have obtained performance rights to this title, please refer to your licensing agreement for important billing and credit requirements.

NATASHA, PIERRE & THE GREAT COMET OF 1812 was commissioned, developed, and first produced by Ars Nova (Jason Eagan, Artistic Director; Jeremy Blocker, Managing Director) in New York City. Opening night was October 16, 2012. The performance was directed by Rachel Chavkin, with sets by Mimi Lien, costumes by Paloma Young, lights by Bradley King, sound by Matthew Hubbs, and orchestrations and music direction by Dave Malloy. The Production Stage Manager was Trisha Henson. The cast was as follows:

NATASHA	Phillipa Soo
PIERRE	Dave Malloy
ANATOLE	Lucas Steele
SONYA	Brittain Ashford
MARYA D.	Amelia Workman
HÉLÈNE	Amber Gray
DOLOKHOV	Nick Choksi
MARY / MAIDSERVANT / OPERA SINGER	Gelsey Bell
ANDREY / BOLKONSKY	Blake DeLong
BALAGA / SERVANT / OPERA SINGER	Paul Pinto

NATASHA, PIERRE & THE GREAT COMET OF 1812 re-opened in New York City Off Broadway at Kazino, a custom-built tent located first in the Meatpacking District and then in Times Square, on May 16, 2013. The production had the same director, designers, and cast, except for the following changes: music direction by Or Matias, choreography by Sam Pinkelton, Grace McLean as **MARYA D.**, Ian Lassiter as **DOLOKHOV**, and Nicholas Belton, Catherine Brookman, Luke Holloway, Azudi Onyejekwe, Mariand Torres, and Lauren Zakrin as **ENSEMBLE**. The Production Stage Manager was Karyn Meek.

NATASHA, PIERRE & THE GREAT COMET OF 1812 opened at A.R.T. in Cambridge, Massachusetts on December 6, 2015. The production was directed by Rachel Chavkin, with choreography by Sam Pinkelton, scenic design by Mimi Lien, costume design by Paloma Young, lighting design by Bradley King, sound design by Matt Hubbs, music direction by Or Matias, and orchestrations by Dave Malloy. The Production Stage Manager was Karyn Meek. The cast was as follows:

NATASHA	Denée Benton
PIERRE	Scott Stangland
ANATOLE	Lucas Steele
SONYA	Brittain Ashford
MARYA D.	Grace McLean

HÉLÈNE..Lilli Cooper
DOLOKHOV ....Nick Choksi
MARY / MAIDSERVANT / OPERA SINGER..............Gelsey Bell
ANDREY / BOLKONSKY .... Nicholas Belton
BALAGA / SERVANT / OPERA SINGER................. Paul Pinto
ENSEMBLE..Sumayya Ali,
   Courtney Bassett, Josh Canfield, Ken Clark, Erica Dorfler, Daniel
   Emond, Lulu Fall, Ashley Pérez Flanagan, Nick Gaswirth, Azudi
   Onyejekwe, Pearl Rhein, Heath Saunders, Katrina Yaukey, Lauren
   Zakrin

NATASHA, PIERRE & THE GREAT COMET OF 1812 opened on Broadway at the Imperial Theatre in New York City on November 14, 2016. The production was directed by Rachel Chavkin, with choreography by Sam Pinkleton, scenic design by Mimi Lien, costume design by Paloma Young, lighting design by Bradley King, sound design by Nicholas Pope, music direction by Or Matias, and orchestrations by Dave Malloy. The Production Stage Manager was Karyn Meek. The cast was as follows:

NATASHA...Denée Benton
PIERRE .... Josh Groban
ANATOLE... Lucas Steele
SONYA..Brittain Ashford
MARYA D.... Grace McLean
HÉLÈNE..Amber Gray
DOLOKHOV ....Nick Choksi
MARY / MAIDSERVANT / OPERA SINGER..............Gelsey Bell
ANDREY / BOLKONSKY .... Nicholas Belton
BALAGA / SERVANT / OPERA SINGER................. Paul Pinto
PIERRE (STANDBY)............................... Scott Stangland
ENSEMBLE............. Sumayya Ali, Courtney Bassett, Josh Canfield,
   Ken Clark, Erica Dorfler, Lulu Fall, Ashley Pérez Flanagan, Paloma
   Garcia-Lee, Nick Gaswirth, Alex Gibson, Billy Joe Kiessling, Mary
   Spencer Knapp, Reed Luplau, Brandt Martinez, Andrew Mayer,
   Azudi Onyejekwe, Pearl Rhein, Heath Saunders, Ani Taj, Cathryn
   Wake, Katrina Yaukey, Lauren Zakrin

CHARACTERS

There's a war going on out there somewhere, and **ANDREY** isn't here.

NATASHA is young; she loves Andrey with all her heart.

SONYA is good; Natasha's cousin and closest friend.

MARYA D. is old-school; a grande dame of Moscow. Natasha's godmother, strict yet kind.

ANATOLE is hot; he spends his money on women and wine.

HÉLÈNE is a slut; Anatole's sister, married to Pierre.

DOLOKHOV is fierce (but not too important); Anatole's friend, a crazy good shot.

OLD PRINCE BOLKONSKY is crazy, and **MARY** is plain; Andrey's family – totally messed up.

BALAGA is just for fun.

And what about **PIERRE**? Dear, bewildered, awkward **PIERRE**?

ENSEMBLE / VARIOUS OTHERS (2f, 2m+)

TIME & SETTING

Various locations in 19th-century Russia. The original production used immersive staging to create a 19th-century Russian dinner club/21st-century New York nightclub atmosphere.

PRODUCTION NOTES

In the original production, actors played many of the instruments. While this is not mandatory, an Instrument Breakdown Guide is included in the rental package.

BOLKONSKY and **ANDREY** should be played by the same actor. **BALAGA** also plays all **SERVANTS** and an **OPERA SINGER**. **MARY** also plays the **MAIDSERVANT** and an **OPERA SINGER**.

NOTE ON THE TRANSLATION

The primary source for the libretto is Aylmer and Louise Maude's 1922 translation; several other translations were also consulted, including those by Anthony Briggs, Richard Pevear & Larissa Volokhonsky, and Constance Garnett.

SYNOPSIS

PROLOGUE

Moscow, 1812, just before Napoleon's invasion of Russia and the burning of the city. As the story begins ("Prologue") we meet "Pierre," a wealthy aristocrat having an existential crisis, living a slothful life of wine, philosophy, and inaction.

PART I

Meanwhile, the young, newly engaged Natasha Rostova and her cousin Sonya arrive in "Moscow" to stay the winter with Marya D., Natasha's godmother, while Natasha waits for her fiancé, Andrey, to return from the war. Marya D. tells Natasha that she must visit her future in-laws, the demented, miserly old Prince Bolkonsky and his spinster daughter, Mary ("The Private and Intimate Life of the House"), to win their affection and secure the marriage, which is critical to the Rostovs' status and fortune. However, Natasha's visit ends in disaster ("Natasha & Bolkonskys"), and she leaves missing Andrey more than ever ("No One Else").

PART II

The next night, Natasha is introduced to decadent Moscow society at "The Opera"; there she meets Anatole, a young officer and notorious rogue ("Natasha & Anatole"); their interaction leaves Natasha feeling confused.

PART III

Anatole, his friend Dolokhov, and Pierre go out drinking; they are met by Hélène, (Pierre's wife and Anatole's sister), who taunts Pierre. Anatole declares his intention to have Natasha, although he is already married. Pierre finds his wife's familiarity with Dolokhov offensive and challenges him to a duel, almost getting himself killed ("The Duel"). Afterward, Pierre reflects on his life ("Dust and Ashes"). Natasha and her family go to church ("Sunday Morning"); later, Hélène arrives and invites Natasha to the ball that night ("Charming"), where Anatole seduces Natasha ("The Ball").

INTERMISSION

PART IV

Natasha and Anatole make plans to elope, and Natasha breaks off her engagement with Andrey ("Letters"). Sonya finds out about the plan and realizes it will mean Natasha's ruin ("Sonya & Natasha"); she determines to stop her at any cost ("Sonya Alone"). That evening Anatole and Dolokhov plan for the elopement ("Preparations") and call on their trusted troika driver, "Balaga," to take them to Natasha's house. However,

"The Abduction" is thwarted at the last moment by Marya D.

PART V

After scolding a grief-stricken Natasha ("In My House"), Marya D. sends out "A Call to Pierre," asking him to help handle the crisis. Pierre kicks Anatole out of Moscow ("Find Anatole" / "Pierre & Anatole"); Natasha poisons herself ("Natasha Very Ill"); Andrey returns. Pierre explains the scandal to him and asks him to be compassionate, but Andrey is unable to forgive ("Pierre & Andrey"). Finally, Pierre visits Natasha ("Pierre & Natasha"). After their meeting, Pierre experiences a moment of enlightenment while seeing "The Great Comet of 1812" in the night sky.

SCENIC BREAKDOWN

PROLOGUE
1. Prologue (Company)
2. Pierre (Aria and Chorus: Pierre, Company)

PART I
Chapter 1
3. Moscow (Trio: Marya D., Natasha, Sonya)
Chapter 2
4. The Private and Intimate Life of the House (Duet: Bolkonsky, Mary)
5. Natasha & Bolkonskys (Trio: Natasha, Mary, Bolkonsky)
6. No One Else (Aria: Natasha)

PART II
Chapter 3
7. The Opera (Company)
8. Natasha & Anatole (Duet: Natasha, Anatole)

PART III
Chapter 4
9. The Duel (Quartet and Chorus: Pierre, Anatole, Dolokhov, Hélène, Company)
10. Dust and Ashes (Aria: Pierre, with Chorus)
Chapter 5
11. Sunday Morning (Trio: Natasha, Sonya, Marya D.)
12. Charming (Aria: Hélène, with Natasha)
Chapter 6
13. The Ball (Duet: Natasha, Anatole)

PART IV
Chapter 7
14. Letters (Company)
Chapter 8
15. Sonya & Natasha (Duet: Sonya, Natasha)
16. Sonya Alone (Aria: Sonya)
Chapter 9
17. Preparations (Duet: Dolokhov, Anatole, with Pierre)
18. Balaga (Trio and Chorus: Balaga, Anatole, Dolokhov, Company)
19. The Abduction (Company)

PART V
Chapter 10
20. In My House (Trio: Marya D., Natasha, Sonya)
21. A Call to Pierre (Duet: Pierre, Marya D., with Chorus)

Chapter 11
  22. Find Anatole (Aria: Pierre, with Natasha, Anatole, Hélène, Chorus)
  23. Pierre & Anatole (Duet: Pierre, Anatole)

Chapter 12
  24. Natasha Very Ill (Aria: Sonya)
  25. Pierre & Andrey (Duet: Pierre, Andrey)

Chapter 13
  26. Pierre & Natasha (Duet: Pierre, Natasha)
  27. The Great Comet of 1812 (Aria and Chorus: Pierre, Company)

FOREWORD

"Have you read *War and Peace*?" Dave and I were strolling across the grass while in residence upstate on our first gig together. We were still getting to know each other and discussing dream projects. He described his experience reading the novel with a former girlfriend; a long-distance activity to keep them united while he was working on a cruise ship. We talked about the scope of the novel, the humor and bitterness with which it depicts this decadent society, the depravity and spiritual regeneration of its characters. Dave strongly identified with Pierre, the supernaturally large, painfully awkward but beloved illegitimate son of the wealthiest man in Russia. Pierre's story is interwoven with the story of Natasha Rostova, and at the center of the novel the two come crashing together when she almost elopes with Anatole Kuragin. In helping to save the reputation and spirits of this young woman, Pierre saves himself.

When you first meet Natasha in the novel, she is a precocious thirteen-year-old dragging a boy into a corner for a stolen kiss. You're immediately drawn to her, as are so many of the men in the book, including Pierre and his tragic best friend, Andrey. She's headstrong and joy-filled and selfish and philosophical. And in creating the production and character, first with Phillipa Soo and then Denée Benton, it became clear that the audience needed to shift constantly between wanting to throttle her and sweep her up in their arms. Pierre is no less complicated; he is an alcoholic and a mystic, and pathetic and graceful. Both are compelling characters not for their nobility, but for their improbability as moral forces. As these two broken souls find each other at the end of this seventy-page sliver, there's a celestial event: the appearance of the comet of 1812 (which actually appeared in 1811 but Tolstoy renamed for narrative effect). Almost immediately after the events depicted in this piece, Napoleon will invade and Moscow will be burned to the ground. Many of the characters won't live much longer. Like the novel, *Natasha, Pierre & The Great Comet of 1812* is about small humans at sea in the vast confusion of history; their pettiness, their mistakes, and their redemption.

Dave has an uncanny ability to see songs where the rest of us see a sentence. He read these pages and he saw an opera. He read a short chapter about a drunken troika driver named Balaga, and saw a number that would unite audience and performers in a shaking, stomping celebration just before the downfall of our heroine. I likely should say he "heard" all this, but one of my favorite things about Dave as a collaborator is that he writes for performance. At the start of our work, alongside discussing the novel, he told the creative team and I about this magical night he'd experienced while traveling in Russia. He'd found a packed underground cafe, and amidst the crush of tables topped with vodka and dumplings, a string trio madly played while the audience rocked out with handmade shakers. He sat next to the viola, and this close-up musical experience got him thinking about distributing the orchestra all around the room so that each audience member would have a unique aural experience.

Our production, from Ars Nova to the Imperial Theatre, grew up from the seeds of this anecdote. The design team and I wrestled with what we needed to tell Tolstoy's story as imagined by Dave. It was clear that we required a fusion of period and contemporary elements, because it's an old story told with new music. Tolstoy mocks opera, along with many other aristocratic affectations. Dave both captures Tolstoy's skepticism and embraces the form, fusing it with the populist modern American musical. His love for the Dirty Projectors and electronica and Joni Mitchell and Russian drinking songs all found their way into the score. This musical eclecticism necessitated that our production make space for the modern world, particularly during "The Duel," in which the theater turned into a full-blown, strobe-lit, nauseous nightclub. But we also couldn't entirely live in the present. It was vital that the audience release into the 19th-century melodrama, in order to empathize with the central characters. Mimi Lien, our scenic designer, did image research of nightclubs around the world. She and Bradley King, our lighting designer, together developed the look of our chandeliers, inspired in part by research into comets, and in part by the starburst chandeliers at the Metropolitan Opera (which felt satisfying to reference). Paloma Young, our costume designer, sketched dress after jean jacket after dress, as we found a balance between period and "folk-punk." Our sound designer, Nick Pope, and his team sat in nearly every seat during tech as they crafted the individual mix each audience member would hear, paralleling Dave's experience with that viola in Moscow.

In his libretto, Dave preserved Tolstoy's iconic narrative voice. The characters sometimes describe each other in endearing or acidic ways, and occasionally they describe themselves as emotions become particularly heightened or unhinged. This narration allowed us to tell joyful, bold-faced lies to the audience again and again in staging. Perhaps my favorite instance of this was the top of the final song, when Pierre sings, "And I get in to my sleigh," but the performer simply climbs the stairs. Because of the narration, the staging was freed to capture the emotional truth of an event, such as a wild troika ride or Natasha becoming intoxicated by Anatole's attention at the opera, vs. needing to literally represent the story.

Comet was a singular experience for most of us; dozens of us made our Broadway debuts with the show, and it was all the more special because that was never the intention when we began development at the tiny-but-mighty Ars Nova in 2011. There's too many memories to list, and too many people to thank individually, from the original cast and band members to the incredible crew at the Imperial Theatre on our closing in September 2017. But I do want to acknowledge our producers, particularly Jason Eagan and Jeremy Blocker and everyone at Ars Nova; Diane Paulus and Diane Borger and everyone at A.R.T.; and Howard and Janet Kagan, who never stopped believing it could and should be experienced in a larger space by more humans.

When I think of the show, I think of the final number. It's one of the few bits of staging that remained basically the same from Ars Nova to Broadway. Pierre sings quietly in a nearly darkened space, barely lit by a single glowing light bulb and wondering where to go. As he wanders on, the choir sings in hushed tones, and the glow quietly spreads to the next bulb and the next, each becoming a glittering star. The light then spreads to the chandeliers, which become dim clusters in the Moscow sky. The ensemble is spread throughout the darkness. Whenever I watched the show, at some point during this song, I would close my eyes. I'd listen to the company and picture myself also wandering, lost and found all at once. And then I would open my eyes as Pierre sees the comet for the first time. The creative team and I talked endlessly about how to "do" the comet, and decided that the simplest gesture was the best: a single bulb on a chandelier that maybe the audience hadn't really considered till now. It felt like this matched the performance event Dave wrote; a whole room united around a single light bulb, and a whole community united around these two fragile humans. During the final violent swell of Dave's score, the light also spreads on this chandelier. It becomes blinding (evoking the atomic history of the Met chandeliers), lighting the entire room, including the audience and the ensemble, all of whom are staring at this symbol of death or new life. And then, as the music finds its quiet last harmony, the chandelier fades back to a single bulb, which then goes black with the wave of the music director's hands.

– Rachel Chavkin

*To Eliza:
my Natasha, my Sonya,
my Andrey, my Anatole,
and my Comet.*

PROLOGUE

1. "PROLOGUE"

(An accordion plays as **ANDREY** *finishes putting on his uniform. He gives a last goodbye to* **NATASHA** *and then leaves.)*

PIERRE.
>THERE'S A WAR GOING ON
>OUT THERE SOMEWHERE
>AND ANDREY ISN'T HERE
>THERE'S A WAR GOING ON
>OUT THERE SOMEWHERE
>AND ANDREY ISN'T HERE

ALL.
>THERE'S A WAR GOING ON
>OUT THERE SOMEWHERE
>AND ANDREY ISN'T HERE
>THERE'S A WAR GOING ON
>OUT THERE SOMEWHERE
>AND ANDREY ISN'T HERE

CONDUCTOR. *Raz dva tri!*

ALL.
>AND THIS IS ALL IN YOUR PROGRAM
>YOU ARE AT THE OPERA
>GONNA HAVE TO STUDY UP A LITTLE BIT
>IF YOU WANNA KEEP WITH THE PLOT
>CUZ IT'S A COMPLICATED RUSSIAN NOVEL
>EVERYONE'S GOT NINE DIFFERENT NAMES
>SO LOOK IT UP IN YOUR PROGRAM
>WE'D APPRECIATE IT, THANKS A LOT

DA DA DA
DA DA DA
DA DA DA

NATASHA!

NATASHA.

NATASHA IS YOUNG
SHE LOVES ANDREY WITH ALL HER HEART

ALL.

SHE LOVES ANDREY WITH ALL HER HEART
NATASHA IS YOUNG
AND ANDREY ISN'T HERE

SONYA.

SONYA IS GOOD
NATASHA'S COUSIN AND CLOSEST FRIEND

ALL.

NATASHA'S COUSIN AND CLOSEST FRIEND
SONYA IS GOOD
NATASHA IS YOUNG
AND ANDREY ISN'T HERE

MARYA D.

MARYA IS OLD-SCHOOL, A GRANDE DAME OF MOSCOW
NATASHA'S GODMOTHER, STRICT YET KIND

ALL.

NATASHA'S GODMOTHER, STRICT YET KIND
MARYA IS OLD-SCHOOL
SONYA IS GOOD
NATASHA IS YOUNG
AND ANDREY ISN'T HERE

AND THIS IS ALL IN YOUR PROGRAM
YOU ARE AT THE OPERA
GONNA HAVE TO STUDY UP A LITTLE BIT
IF YOU WANNA KEEP WITH THE PLOT
CUZ IT'S A COMPLICATED RUSSIAN NOVEL
EVERYONE'S GOT NINE DIFFERENT NAMES
SO LOOK IT UP IN YOUR PROGRAM
WE'D APPRECIATE IT, THANKS A LOT
DA DA DA

DA DA DA
DA DA DA
ANATOLE!

ANATOLE.
ANATOLE IS HOT
HE SPENDS HIS MONEY ON WOMEN AND WINE

ALL.
HE SPENDS HIS MONEY ON WOMEN AND WINE
ANATOLE IS HOT
MARYA IS OLD-SCHOOL
SONYA IS GOOD
NATASHA IS YOUNG
AND ANDREY ISN'T HERE

HÉLÈNE.
HÉLÈNE IS A SLUT
ANATOLE'S SISTER, MARRIED TO PIERRE

ALL.
ANATOLE'S SISTER, MARRIED TO PIERRE
HÉLÈNE IS A SLUT
ANATOLE IS HOT
MARYA IS OLD-SCHOOL
SONYA IS GOOD
NATASHA IS YOUNG
AND ANDREY ISN'T HERE

DOLOKHOV.
DOLOKHOV IS FIERCE, BUT NOT TOO IMPORTANT
ANATOLE'S FRIEND, A CRAZY GOOD SHOT

ALL.
ANATOLE'S FRIEND, A CRAZY GOOD SHOT
DOLOKHOV IS FIERCE
HÉLÈNE IS A SLUT
ANATOLE IS HOT
MARYA IS OLD-SCHOOL
SONYA IS GOOD
NATASHA IS YOUNG
AND ANDREY ISN'T HERE

CHANDELIERS AND CAVIAR

THE WAR CAN'T TOUCH US HERE

MINOR CHARACTERS!

BOLKONSKY.

OLD PRINCE BOLKONSKY IS CRAZY

MARY.

AND MARY IS PLAIN

MARY & BOLKONSKY.

ANDREY'S FAMILY, TOTALLY MESSED UP

BALAGA.

AND BALAGA'S JUST FOR FUN!

ALL.

BALAGA'S JUST FOR FUN!

BALAGA IS FUN
BOLKONSKY IS CRAZY
MARY IS PLAIN
DOLOKHOV IS FIERCE
HÉLÈNE IS A SLUT
ANATOLE IS HOT
MARYA IS OLD-SCHOOL
SONYA IS GOOD
NATASHA IS YOUNG
AND ANDREY ISN'T HERE

AND WHAT ABOUT PIERRE?
DEAR, BEWILDERED AND AWKWARD PIERRE?
WHAT ABOUT PIERRE?
RICH, UNHAPPILY MARRIED PIERRE?
WHAT ABOUT PIERRE?
WHAT ABOUT PIERRE?
WHAT ABOUT PIERRE?

2. "PIERRE"

PIERRE.
>IT'S DAWNED ON ME SUDDENLY
>AND FOR NO OBVIOUS REASON
>THAT I CAN'T GO ON
>LIVING AS I AM
>
>THE ZEST OF LIFE HAS VANISHED
>ONLY THE SKELETON REMAINS
>UNEXPECTEDLY VILE
>I USED TO BE BETTER

CHORUS.
>AH...
>
>OH PIERRE! OUR MERRY FEASTING CRANK
>OUR MOST DEAR, MOST KIND, MOST SMART
>AND ECCENTRIC
>A WARM-HEARTED RUSSIAN OF THE OLD SCHOOL
>HIS PURSE IS ALWAYS EMPTY
>CUZ IT'S OPEN TO ALL
>OH PIERRE
>JUST ONE OF A HUNDRED SAD OLD MEN
>LIVING OUT THEIR FINAL DAYS IN MOSCOW

PIERRE.
>I DRINK TOO MUCH
>RIGHT NOW, MY FRIEND FIGHTS AND BLEEDS
>AND I SIT AT HOME AND READ
>HOURS AT A TIME
>HOURS AT MY SCREEN
>ANYTHING, ANYTHING
>ABANDONED TO DISTRACTION
>IN ORDER TO FORGET
>WE WASTE OUR LIVES
>DROWNING IN WINE
>
>I NEVER THOUGHT THAT I'D
>END UP LIKE THIS
>I USED TO BE BETTER
>
>AND THE WOMEN THEY ALL PITY ME

CUZ I'M MARRIED
BUT NOT IN LOVE
FROZEN AT THE CENTER

WOMEN.

IL EST CHARMANT; IL N'A PAS DE SEXE
HE IS CHARMING; HE HAS NO SEX

CHORUS.

OH PIERRE! OUR MERRY FEASTING CRANK
OUR MOST DEAR, MOST KIND, MOST SMART
AND ECCENTRIC
A WARM-HEARTED RUSSIAN OF THE OLD SCHOOL
HIS PURSE IS ALWAYS EMPTY
CUZ IT'S OPEN TO ALL
OH PIERRE
JUST ONE OF A HUNDRED SAD OLD MEN
LIVING OUT THEIR FINAL DAYS IN MOSCOW

PIERRE.

THERE'S A RINGING IN MY HEAD
THERE'S A SICKNESS IN THE WORLD
AND EVERYONE KNOWS
BUT PRETENDS THAT THEY DON'T SEE
"OH, I'LL SORT IT OUT LATER"
BUT LATER NEVER COMES

PIERRE & MEN.

AND HOW MANY MEN BEFORE
GOOD RUSSIAN MEN
BELIEVING IN GOODNESS AND TRUTH

PIERRE.

ENTERED THAT DOOR
WITH ALL THEIR TEETH AND HAIR
AND LEFT IT TOOTHLESS AND BALD

YOU EMPTY AND STUPID
CONTENTED FELLOWS
SATISFIED WITH YOUR PLACE
I'M DIFFERENT FROM YOU
I'M DIFFERENT FROM YOU
I STILL WANT TO DO SOMETHING

OR DO YOU STRUGGLE TOO?
I PITY YOU, I PITY ME, I PITY YOU
I PITY YOU, I PITY ME, I PITY YOU

CHORUS.
AH…

PART I

Chapter 1

3. "MOSCOW"

PIERRE. *Raz dva tri!*

> (**NATASHA** *and* **SONYA** *arrive on sleighs.*)

NATASHA.
> MARYA DMITRYEVNA AKHROSIMOVA

MARYA D.
> COUNTESS NATALYA ILYINICHNA ROSTOVA

NATASHA.
> YOU MUST CALL ME NATASHA

SONYA.
> MARYA DMITRYEVNA AKHROSIMOVA

MARYA D.
> SOFIA ALEXANDROVNA ROSTOVA

SONYA.
> YOU MUST CALL ME SONYA

MARYA D.
> WELCOME
> WELCOME TO MOSCOW
> WHERE FADED AND FADING PRINCESSES LIVE
> I'LL TAKE YOU WHERE YOU MUST GO
> PET YOU A BIT
> AND I'LL SCOLD YOU A BIT
> MY GODDAUGHTER, MY FAVORITE, NATASHA
> I WILL TOUCH YOU ON THE CHEEK

NATASHA & SONYA.
>MY COUSIN AND I
>ARE SO PLEASED TO BE WITH YOU
>WHILE WE WAIT ON OUR FIANCÉS
>FIGHTING IN THE WAR

MARYA D.
>BRING IN THEIR THINGS!
>WHAT ARE YOU DAWDLING FOR?
>GET THE SAMOVAR READY!
>YOU'RE HALF FROZEN, I'M SURE!
>BRING SOME RUM FOR THE TEA!
>SONYUSHKA BONJOUR
>AND NATASHA MY DARLING
>YOU'VE GROWN PLUMPER AND PRETTIER

NATASHA.
>MY CHEEKS ARE GLOWING FROM THE COLD

SONYA.
>SHE SAID
>GAZING AT MARYA WITH KIND, GLITTERING EYES

MARYA D.
>WELCOME
>WELCOME TO MOSCOW
>SCRUFFY AND COZY
>LIKE AN OLD DRESSING GOWN

SONYA.
>COUNTESS NATALYA

NATASHA.
>SOFIA ALEXANDROVNA

SONYA.
>HOW BEAUTIFUL YOU LOOKED IN THE SNOW

NATASHA.
>COUSIN DEAR I LOVE YOU
>TRUST NO ONE BUT YOU
>BUT I CAN'T BEAR THIS WAITING
>I CRY AND I CRY
>ANDREY WHERE ARE YOU?
>I WANT HIM NOW, AT ONCE

TO EMBRACE HIM AND CLING TO HIM
NO ONE CAN UNDERSTAND

I LOVE HIM
I KNOW HIM
HE LOVES ME ONLY
HE'LL COME HOME ONE DAY
AND TAKE ME AWAY
I WANT NOTHING MORE
I WANT NOTHING MORE
HMMM...

MARYA D.

FIRST THING TOMORROW TO MADAME CHAMBORD'S
DRESSES, DRESSES, WE'LL BUY WHAT WE CAN AFFORD
THEN DINNER AND A GAME OF BOSTON
THEN YOU'LL READ TO ME WHILE I KNIT!
HOW WONDERFUL TO HAVE YOU HERE
INSTEAD OF THESE GOSSIPS AND CRYBABIES

NATASHA & SONYA.

YOU'LL TAKE US WHERE WE MUST GO
PET US A BIT
AND SCOLD US A BIT

SONYA.

HER GODDAUGHTER, HER FAVORITE, NATASHA
SHE WILL TOUCH YOU ON THE CHEEK

(**SONYA** *leaves.*)

MARYA D.

WELL, NOW WE'LL TALK
I CONGRATULATE YOU AND ANDREY
YOU'VE HOOKED A FINE FELLOW!
ONE OF THE FINEST MATCHES IN ALL OF RUSSIA
I AM GLAD AND RELIEVED
HE'LL BE THE FAMILY'S SAVING GRACE

NATASHA.

I BLUSH HAPPILY

MARYA D.

BUT HIS FATHER, PRINCE BOLKONSKY,
MUCH DISLIKES HIS SON'S MARRYING

THE OLD FELLOW'S CROTCHETY!
OF COURSE PRINCE ANDREY'S NOT A CHILD
BUT IT'S NOT NICE TO ENTER A FAMILY
AGAINST A FATHER'S WILL
ONE WANTS TO DO IT PEACEFULLY AND LOVINGLY
BUT YOU'RE A CLEVER GIRL
JUST BE KIND TO ANDREY'S SISTER
AND WHEN THE SISTER LOVES YOU
SO WILL THE FATHER
AND ALL WILL BE WELL

Chapter 2

4. "THE PRIVATE AND INTIMATE LIFE OF THE HOUSE"

BOLKONSKY.
>I'VE AGED
>I'VE AGED SO VERY MUCH
>I FALL ASLEEP AT THE TABLE
>MY NAPKIN DROPS TO THE FLOOR
>
>I'M FULL OF CHILDISH VANITIES
>I FORGET THINGS
>AND I LIVE IN THE PAST
>I'VE AGED SO VERY MUCH
>
>PEOPLE ENJOY ME THOUGH
>I COME IN FOR TEA IN MY OLD-FASHIONED COAT AND POWDERED WIG
>AND I TELL STORIES
>AND UTTER SCATHING CRITIQUES
>THIS STERN, SHREWD OLD MAN
>A RELIC OF THE PAST CENTURY
>WITH HIS GENTLE DAUGHTER
>SUCH A MAJESTIC AND AGREEABLE SPECTACLE

MARY.
>BUT BESIDES THE COUPLE OF HOURS DURING WHICH WE HAVE GUESTS
>THERE ARE ALSO TWENTY-TWO HOURS IN THE DAY
>DURING WHICH THE PRIVATE AND INTIMATE LIFE OF THE HOUSE CONTINUES

BOLKONSKY.
>BRING ME MY SLIPPERS

MARY.
>YES FATHER YES FATHER

BOLKONSKY.
>BRING ME MY WINE

MARY.
>YES FATHER YES FATHER

BOLKONSKY.
>IF YOU'RE NOT TOO BUSY
>FIDDLING WITH YOUR INCENSE AND ICONS?

MARY.
>NO FATHER NO FATHER
>AND I HAVE NO FRIENDS
>NO, NEVER GO ANYWHERE
>NEVER INVITED
>FOR WHO WOULD TAKE CARE OF HIM

BOLKONSKY.
>I CAN HURT YOU

BOTH.
>I CAN HURT YOU

MARY.
>BUT I NEVER EVER EVER EVER WOULD
>NO FATHER
>I LOVE YOU FATHER
>
>AND TIME MOVES ON
>AND MY FATE SLIPS PAST
>AND NOTHING EVER HAPPENS TO ME
>AND COUNTESS NATALYA ROSTOVA IS COMING FOR TEA

NATASHA.
>I KNOW THEY'LL LIKE ME
>EVERYONE HAS ALWAYS LIKED ME

BOLKONSKY.
>NATASHA IS YOUNG
>AND WORTHLESS AND DUMB

MARY.
>AND TIME MOVES ON
>AND MY FATE SLIPS PAST
>IS THIS ALL I'LL MAKE OF MY LIFE?
>WILL I NEVER BE HAPPY?
>WILL I NEVER BE ANYONE'S WIFE?

BOLKONSKY.
>AH, WHAT'S THIS? A YOUNG SUITOR!

AH, COME IN, COME IN
BUT DON'T SIT DOWN, DON'T SIT DOWN
I'M COLD TO YOU
YES I'M MEAN TO YOU

NOW BE GONE, BE GONE, BE GONE!
AND DON'T COME BACK!

OH, MAYBE I'LL MARRY SOMEONE MYSELF
SOME CHEAP FRENCH THING
OH THAT OFFENDS YOU DOES IT?
AH, COME IN MY DEAR
COME IN MY DEAR, COME IN

MARY.
AND HE DRAWS HER TO HIM
AND HE KISSES HER HAND
EMBRACES HER AFFECTIONATELY
AND I FLUSH AND RUN OUT OF THE ROOM

BOLKONSKY.
COME BACK HERE
LET AN OLD MAN HAVE HIS FUN

MARY.
BUT SHE'S USING YOU PAPA
WANTS YOUR MONEY PAPA!
TO TAKE ADVANTAGE OF YOUR WEAKNESS LIKE THAT
IT'S DISGUSTING
MY VOICE BREAKS

BOLKONSKY.
IT'S MY MONEY AND I'LL THROW IT WHERE I WANT
NOT AT YOU!
AND NOT AT ANDREY'S HARLOT!

INSOLENT GIRL!
INSOLENT GIRL!
WHERE –
WHERE –

WHERE ARE MY GLASSES?
WHERE ARE THEY?
WHERE ARE MY GLASSES?

OH GOD –
OH GOD I'M FRIGHTENED
OH GOD I'VE AGED SO VERY MUCH

WHERE ARE MY GLASSES?
WHERE ARE MY GLASSES?

MARY.
THEY ARE THERE UPON HIS HEAD
THE PRIDE OF SACRIFICE
GATHERS IN MY SOUL

AND HE FORGETS THINGS
HE FALLS ASLEEP AT THE TABLE
HIS NAPKIN DROPS TO THE FLOOR
HIS SHAKING HEAD
SINKS OVER HIS PLATE

HE IS OLD AND FEEBLE
AND I DARE TO JUDGE HIM
I DISGUST MYSELF
I DISGUST MYSELF

5. "NATASHA & BOLKONSKYS"

SERVANT.
> MAY I PRESENT THE COUNTESS
> NATALYA ROSTOVA

MARY.
> OH
> OH, HELLO
> WON'T YOU COME IN?

NATASHA.
> HELLO

>> (**NATASHA** and **MARY** *awkwardly move to a table in silence.*)

MARY.
> AND FROM THE FIRST GLANCE I DO NOT LIKE NATASHA
> TOO FASHIONABLY DRESSED
> FRIVOLOUS AND VAIN
> HER BEAUTY, YOUTH, AND HAPPINESS
> MY BROTHER'S LOVE FOR HER
> AND MY FATHER –

BOLKONSKY.
> I DO NOT WISH TO SEE HER!

MARY.
> I KNOW AT ANY MOMENT HE MIGHT INDULGE IN SOME FREAK

NATASHA.
> I'M SORRY THE PRINCE IS STILL AILING

BOLKONSKY.
> SONGSTRESS!

NATASHA.
> I AM NOT AFRAID OF ANYONE
>
> BUT SUCH HESITATION
> SUCH UNNATURAL MANNERS
>
> AND FROM THE FIRST GLANCE I DO NOT LIKE PRINCESS MARY
> TOO PLAIN AND AFFECTED

    INSOLENT AND DRY
    I SHRINK INTO MYSELF
    ASSUME AN OFFHAND AIR

MARY.
    WHICH ALIENATES ME STILL MORE

NATASHA & MARY.
    CONSTRAINED AND STRAINED
    CONSTRAINED AND STRAINED
    CONSTRAINED AND STRAINED
    IRKSOME
    IRKSOME

       (**BOLKONSKY** *enters in his underthings.*)

BOLKONSKY.
    OH!

MARY.
    PAPA!

BOLKONSKY.
    OH, SO THIS IS NATASHA
    NOT MUCH TO LOOK AT
    SAYS THE MEAN OLD MAN IN HIS UNDERTHINGS
    I NEVER DRESS FOR CHILDREN OR PEASANTS
    SAYS THE MEAN OLD MAN IN HIS UNDERTHINGS

MARY.
    AND HE LOOKED AT HER ONCE
    HEAD TO TOE
    AND LEFT MUTTERING

NATASHA.
    I MUST TAKE MY LEAVE

MARY.
    PLEASE WAIT –

    DEAR NATALIE
    I WANT YOU TO KNOW HOW GLAD I AM MY BROTHER HAS
        FOUND HAPPINESS

NATASHA.
    IS THAT THE TRUTH?
    I THINK IT IS NOT CONVENIENT TO SPEAK OF THAT NOW

DEAR PRINCESS
MARY.
SHE SAID
WITH SUCH DIGNITY AND COLDNESS
NATASHA.
WHAT HAVE I SAID, WHAT HAVE I DONE?
CRYING LIKE A CHILD
OH, THEY WERE SO AWFUL!
OH, IT ALL HURTS SO TERRIBLY
ANDREY
WHERE ARE YOU?

6. "NO ONE ELSE"

NATASHA.
>THE MOON –
>
>FIRST TIME I HEARD YOUR VOICE
>MOONLIGHT BURST INTO THE ROOM
>AND I SAW YOUR EYES
>AND I SAW YOUR SMILE
>AND THE WORLD OPENED WIDE
>AND THE WORLD WAS INSIDE OF ME
>
>AND I CATCH MY BREATH
>AND I LAUGH AND BLUSH
>AND I HEAR GUITARS
>YOU ARE SO GOOD FOR ME
>
>I LOVE YOU I LOVE YOU I LOVE YOU I LOVE YOU
>I LOVE YOU
>
>OH THE MOON
>OH THE SNOW IN THE MOONLIGHT
>AND YOUR CHILDLIKE EYES
>AND YOUR DISTANT SMILE
>I'LL NEVER BE THIS HAPPY AGAIN
>YOU AND I
>AND NO ONE ELSE
>
>WE'VE DONE THIS ALL BEFORE
>WE WERE ANGELS ONCE
>DON'T YOU REMEMBER?
>JOY AND LIFE
>INSIDE OUR SOULS,
>AND NOBODY KNOWS
>JUST YOU AND ME
>IT'S OUR SECRET
>
>THIS WINTER SKY
>HOW CAN ANYONE SLEEP?
>THERE WAS NEVER SUCH A NIGHT BEFORE!
>I FEEL LIKE PUTTING MY ARMS ROUND MY KNEES
>AND SQUEEZING TIGHT AS POSSIBLE

AND FLYING AWAY
LIKE THIS...

OH THE MOON
OH THE SNOW IN THE MOONLIGHT
AND YOUR CHILDLIKE EYES
AND YOUR DISTANT SMILE
I'LL NEVER BE THIS HAPPY AGAIN
YOU AND I
YOU AND I
YOU AND I
AND NO ONE ELSE

MAYBE HE'LL COME TODAY
MAYBE HE CAME ALREADY
AND HE'S SITTING IN THE DRAWING ROOM
AND I SIMPLY FORGOT

PART II

Chapter 3

7. "THE OPERA"

MARYA D.
> THE OPERA, THE OPERA!
> STOP MOONING AND MOANING, WE'LL MISS THE CURTAIN!

SERVANT.
> LADIES
> WELCOME TO THE OPERA

SONYA.
> BARE ARMS AND SHOULDERS
> BRILLIANT UNIFORMS
> PEARLS AND SILK
> GLITTERING BEFORE OUR EYES
> FEMININE ENVY
> A WHOLE CROWD OF MEMORIES
> DESIRES AND EMOTIONS
> NATASHA, SMOOTH YOUR GOWN

CHORUS.
> NATASHA, SMOOTH YOUR GOWN

NATASHA.
> LOOKING IN THE GLASS
> I SEE I AM PRETTY
> NOT A GIRL ANYMORE
> I'VE NEVER FELT LIKE THIS BEFORE
>
> HUNDREDS OF EYES
> LOOKING AT MY BARE ARMS

MY BARE ARMS AND NECK
MY BARE ARMS AND SHOULDERS

CHORUS.
THE TWO REMARKABLY PRETTY GIRLS
HAD NOT BEEN SEEN IN MOSCOW IN MANY YEARS
EVERYBODY KNEW VAGUELY OF NATASHA'S ENGAGEMENT
ONE OF THE FINEST MATCHES IN ALL OF RUSSIA

SONYA.
LOOK, THERE'S ALEXEY, HOME FROM THE WAR AT LAST

MARYA D.
HE HAS CHANGED
DEAR ME, MICHAEL KIRILOVICH HAS GROWN STILL STOUTER!

CHORUS.
THERE'S BORIS AND JULIE, ENGAGED
AND ANNA MIKHAYLOVNA, WHAT A HEADDRESS SHE HAS ON!

HÉLÈNE.
AND IS THAT NATASHA?

CHORUS.
AND IS THAT NATASHA
AND IS THAT NATASHA

NATASHA.
THEY ARE LOOKING AT ME
THEY ARE TALKING ABOUT ME!
THEY ALL LIKE ME SO MUCH
THE WOMEN ENVIOUS
THE MEN CALMING THEIR JEALOUSY

SERVANT.
ANNOUNCING FEDYA DOLOKHOV
HE DOMINATES MOSCOW'S MOST BRILLIANT YOUNG MEN
HE STANDS IN FULL VIEW,
WELL AWARE HE'S ATTRACTING ATTENTION
YET AS MUCH AT EASE AS THOUGH HE WERE IN HIS OWN ROOM

MARYA D.
DOLOKHOV WAS IN THE CAUCASUS

AND HE KILLED THE SHAH'S BROTHER!
NOW ALL THE MOSCOW LADIES ARE MAD ABOUT HIM
DOLOKHOV THE ASSASSIN!

SERVANT.

ANNOUNCING COUNTESS HÉLÈNE BEZUKHOVA
THE QUEEN OF SOCIETY
BEAUTIFUL, BARELY CLOTHED
PLUMP BARE SHOULDERS, AND MUCH EXPOSED NECK
ROUND WHICH SHE WEARS A DOUBLE STRING OF PEARLS

CHORUS.

HÉLÈNE AND DOLOKHOV, ARM IN ARM
PIERRE THE CUCKOLD SITS AT HOME
PIERRE THE CUCKOLD SITS AT HOME
THE POOR MAN

PIERRE.

NO, I AM ENJOYING MYSELF AT HOME THIS EVENING

NATASHA.

OH, THAT NECK
OH, THOSE PEARLS

HÉLÈNE.

SO BEAUTIFUL
WHAT A CHARMING YOUNG GIRL
SO ENCHANTING

NATASHA.

I BLUSH SCARLET

MARYA D.

COUNTESS BEZUKHOVA, PIERRE'S WIFE
HAVE YOU BEEN HERE LONG?
AND WHERE IS DEAR PIERRE?
HE NEVER USED TO FORGET US

NATASHA.

YES PIERRE, THAT GOOD MAN
A LITTLE SAD, A LITTLE STOUT
HE MUST COME VISIT US

HÉLÈNE.

I WILL IMPLORE HIM TO DO SO

MARYA D.
>THERE'S A WOMAN ONE SHOULD STAY FAR AWAY FROM
>
>NOW NATASHA
>THE CURTAIN RISES

CHORUS.
>THE CURTAIN RISES

NATASHA.
>EVERYONE IN THE BOXES AND THE STALLS BECAME SILENT
>ALL THE MEN, OLD AND YOUNG, IN UNIFORM AND EVENING DRESS
>ALL THE WOMEN IN THE HALL
>WITH GEMS ON THEIR BARE FLESH
>TURNED THEIR WHOLE ATTENTION
>WITH CURIOSITY TO THE STAGE

>>*(Two **SINGERS** perform a scene from an avant-garde opera. It is grotesque and amazing.)*

>GROTESQUE AND AMAZING
>I CANNOT FOLLOW THE OPERA
>OR EVEN LISTEN TO THE MUSIC
>I SEE PAINTED CARDBOARD
>QUEERLY DRESSED ACTORS
>MOVING AND SINGING SO STRANGELY IN THE LIGHTS
>SO FALSE AND UNNATURAL
>I'M ASHAMED AND AMUSED
>AND EVERYONE ELSE SEEMS OBLIVIOUS
>YES EVERYONE FEIGNS DELIGHT

SONYA.
>AND FEELING THE FLOOD OF BRILLIANT LIGHTS
>THE WARM PERFUMED AIR HEATED BY THE CROWD
>NATASHA LITTLE BY LITTLE
>BEGAN TO PASS INTO A STATE OF INTOXICATION

>>*(**NATASHA** joins the singers in the opera.)*

NATASHA.
>OH I'D TICKLE YOU ALL IF I COULD
>OH I'D TICKLE YOU ALL IF I COULD

SONYA.
>AND THEN
>A RUSH OF COLD AIR

NATASHA & SONYA.
>AN EXCEPTIONALLY HANDSOME MAN WALKED IN
>WITH A CONFIDENT YET COURTEOUS AIR

HÉLÈNE.
>THIS WAS HÉLÈNE'S BROTHER
>ANATOLE KURAGIN
>HE MOVED WITH A SWAGGER
>WHICH WOULD HAVE BEEN RIDICULOUS
>HAD HE NOT BEEN SO GOOD-LOOKING
>AND THOUGH IT WAS THE MIDDLE OF THE ACT
>HE WALKED RIGHT DOWN THE AISLE
>HIS SWORD AND SPURS JANGLING
>HIS HANDSOME PERFUMED HEAD HELD HIGH
>AND HE LOOKED RIGHT AT NATASHA

ANATOLE.
>*MAIS CHARMANTE*

HÉLÈNE.
>AND HE TOOK HIS PLACE IN THE FRONT ROW NEXT TO DOLOKHOV

NATASHA.
>HOW HANDSOME HE IS
>HOW INTOXICATING

SONYA.
>IN THE SECOND ACT THERE WERE TOMBSTONES
>THE MOON OVER THE FOOTLIGHTS
>HORNS AND CONTRABASS
>BLACK CLOAKS AND DAGGERS IN THEIR HANDS

NATASHA.
>I TURN AROUND AGAIN AND OUR EYES MEET
>HE GAZES STRAIGHT INTO MY EYES
>HE IS TALKING ABOUT ME

SONYA.
>CANDLES BURNING
>A CRIMSON THRONE

THE TSAR WAILS A MOURNFUL TUNE
THEY ALL WAVE THEIR ARMS
AND EVERYBODY CHEERS
"BRAVO, BRAVO!"

NATASHA.
EVERY TIME I LOOK AT HIM
HE'S LOOKING AT ME
EVERY TIME I LOOK AT HIM
HE'S LOOKING AT ME
EVERY TIME I LOOK AT HIM

SONYA.
A TERRIBLE NOISE, A CLATTER IN THE CROWD
A STORM OF CHROMATIC SCALES AND DIMINISHED
    SEVENTHS
WITH RAPTUROUS FACES EVERYONE WAS SHOUTING
SCREAMING AND SHOUTING, "BRAVO!"

CHORUS.
BRAVO, BRAVO
BRAVO, BRAVO
BRAVO, BRAVO

SONYA.
AND THEN
A RUSH OF COLD AIR
AND ANATOLE ENTERED THE BOX

8. "NATASHA & ANATOLE"

ANATOLE.
>I HAVE LONG WISHED TO HAVE THIS HAPPINESS
>EVER SINCE THE NARYSHKINS' BALL
>WHERE I HAD THE WELL-REMEMBERED PLEASURE OF
> SEEING YOU
>HOW DO YOU LIKE THE PERFORMANCE?
>LAST WEEK SEMONOVA FELL DOWN ON THE STAGE

NATASHA.
>HE IS SENSIBLE AND SIMPLE
>BOLD AND NATURAL
>SO STRANGE AND AGREEABLE
>THERE IS NOTHING FORMIDABLE
>HIS SMILE IS MOST NAIVE
>CHEERFUL AND GOOD-NATURED
>AND HE'S AS HANDSOME UP CLOSE AS AT A DISTANCE
>AND HE'S AS HANDSOME UP CLOSE AS AT A DISTANCE

ANATOLE.
>AND DO YOU KNOW, NATASHA
>WE ARE HAVING A COSTUME TOURNAMENT SOON
>YOU OUGHT TO COME, PLEASE COME!

NATASHA.
>OH –

ANATOLE.
>YOU OUGHT TO COME, PLEASE COME!

NATASHA.
>OH I –

ANATOLE.
>AND I NEVER REMOVE MY SMILING EYES
>FROM YOUR FACE, YOUR NECK, YOUR BARE ARMS
>AND I NEVER REMOVE MY SMILING EYES
>FROM YOUR FACE, YOUR NECK, YOUR BARE ARMS

NATASHA.
>I KNOW FOR CERTAIN THAT HE IS TAKEN WITH ME
>I KNOW FOR CERTAIN THAT HE IS ENRAPTURED BY ME
>I FEEL HIM LOOKING AT MY SHOULDERS

MY FACE, MY NECK, MY BARE ARMS

ANATOLE.

AND I LOOK YOU IN THE EYE

NATASHA & ANATOLE.

AND I LOOK YOU IN THE EYE

NATASHA.

AND LOOKING INTO HIS EYES
I AM FRIGHTENED
THERE'S NOT THAT BARRIER OF MODESTY
I'VE ALWAYS FELT WITH MEN
I FEEL SO TERRIBLY NEAR
I FEAR THAT HE MAY SEIZE ME FROM BEHIND
AND KISS ME ON THE NECK

HOW DO YOU LIKE MOSCOW?

ANATOLE.

AT FIRST I DID NOT LIKE IT MUCH
BECAUSE WHAT MAKES A TOWN PLEASANT
CE SONT LES JOLIES FEMMES
ISN'T THAT SO?
BUT NOW I LIKE IT VERY MUCH INDEED
DO COME TO THE COSTUME TOURNAMENT COUNTESS
DO COME!
YOU WILL BE THE PRETTIEST THERE
YOU WILL BE THE PRETTIEST THERE
DO COME, DEAR COUNTESS, AND GIVE ME THIS FLOWER
   AS A PLEDGE

WE ARE SPEAKING OF MOST ORDINARY THINGS

NATASHA.

YET I FEEL CLOSER TO YOU THAN I'VE EVER FELT WITH
   ANY OTHER MAN
NO ONE ELSE IS HERE
NO ONE ELSE CAN SEE US
YOUR EYES
YOUR EYES
YOUR EYES
OH YOUR EYES

ANATOLE.
>IT'S ALL RIGHT, NATASHA, I'M HERE

NATASHA & ANATOLE.
>SO NEAR
>NOTHING BETWEEN US
>
>SMILE AT ME
>THERE IS NOTHING BETWEEN US

PART III

Chapter 4

9. "THE DUEL"

(**ANATOLE** *leaves the opera and heads home to Pierre's house.*)

ANATOLE.
GOOD EVENING PIERRE
STUDYING?

PIERRE.
YES. HOW WAS THE OPERA?

ANATOLE.
LOVELY
NATALYA ROSTOVA WAS THERE

PIERRE.
OH, OH DEAR ANDREY'S BETROTHED?
I HAVE KNOWN HER FAMILY FOR YEARS
AND LONG CARRIED AFFECTION FOR HER

ANATOLE.
YES, CHARMING
LOOK, DOLOKHOV'S COMING ROUND AND WE ARE OFF TO THE CLUB
WILL YOU COME OLD MAN?

PIERRE.
I WILL COME

ANATOLE.
LEND ME FIFTY RUBLES?

*(**DOLOKHOV** arrives with many bottles of vodka.)*

DOLOKHOV.
>DRINK DRINK
>GONNA DRINK TONIGHT
>GONNA DRINK TONIGHT
>GONNA DRINK
>GONNA DRINK
>GONNA DRINK TONIGHT
>GONNA DRINK TONIGHT
>GONNA DRINK TONIGHT
>GONNA

DOLOKHOV, ANATOLE & PIERRE.
>DRINK DRINK
>GONNA DRINK TONIGHT
>GONNA DRINK TONIGHT
>GONNA
>GONNA DRINK
>GONNA DRINK TONIGHT
>GONNA DRINK TONIGHT
>GONNA DRINK TONIGHT

(They drink and dance.)

ALL. *Raz dva tri!*
>DRINK WITH ME MY LOVE
>FOR THERE'S FIRE IN THE SKY
>AND THERE'S ICE ON THE GROUND
>EITHER WAY MY SOUL WILL DIE
>WHOA…

PIERRE.
>THE DOCTORS WARN ME
>THAT WITH MY CORPULENCE

A FEW CLUBBERS.
>CORPULENCE

PIERRE.
>VODKA AND WINE ARE DANGEROUS FOR ME
>BUT I DRINK A GREAT DEAL

ONLY QUITE AT EASE
AFTER POURING SEVERAL GLASSES
MECHANICALLY INTO MY LARGE MOUTH

ALL.
THEN I FEEL
A PLEASANT WARMTH IN MY BODY
A SENTIMENTAL ATTACHMENT TO MY FELLOW MEN

(**HÉLÈNE** *arrives and sidles up to* **DOLOKHOV**.)

HÉLÈNE.
KEEP DRINKING OLD MAN

ANATOLE & DOLOKHOV.
KEEP DRINKING OLD MAN

HÉLÈNE, ANATOLE & DOLOKHOV.
DRINK THE WHOLE NIGHT THROUGH
KEEP DRINKING OLD MAN

ALL.
KEEP DRINKING OLD MAN
DRINK THE WHOLE NIGHT THROUGH
KEEP DRINKING OLD MAN

(**PIERRE** *continues to drink, too much.*)

ANATOLE.
NATASHA, NATASHA
HER ARMS, HER SHOULDERS
HER NECK, HER FEET

HÉLÈNE.
THE AIR OF A CONNOISSEUR

ANATOLE.
I WILL MAKE LOVE TO HER

DOLOKHOV.
BETTER NOT, MONSIEUR
SHE'S FIRST-RATE
BUT NOTHING BUT TROUBLE

DOLOKHOV & HÉLÈNE.
BETTER WAIT 'TIL SHE'S MARRIED

DOLOKHOV.
ANATOLE IS A MARRIED MAN

A FACT KNOWN ONLY TO HIS INTIMATES
A POLISH LANDOWNER OF SOME SMALL MEANS
HAD FORCED HIM TO MARRY HIS DAUGHTER

ANATOLE.
NEVERMIND ABOUT THAT NOW
IT DOESN'T MATTER, I DON'T GIVE A DAMN
JUST AS A DUCK IS MADE TO SWIM IN WATER
GOD HAS MADE ME AS I AM
ALL I CARE FOR IS GAIETY AND WOMEN
AND THERE'S NO DISHONOR IN THAT
AS LONG AS THERE'S MONEY AND VODKA
I'LL KEEP A FEATHER IN MY HAT

ALL.
WHOA...

PIERRE.
I USED TO LOVE
I USED TO LOVE
I USED TO BE BETTER

CHORUS.
KEEP DRINKING OLD MAN

HÉLÈNE.
YES DRINK DRINK DRINK
GOD, TO THINK I MARRIED A MAN LIKE YOU

PIERRE.
DON'T SPEAK TO ME, WIFE
THERE IS SOMETHING INSIDE ME

HÉLÈNE.
DOLOKHOV POUR ME ANOTHER

PIERRE.
SOMETHING TERRIBLE AND MONSTROUS

DOLOKHOV.
HERE'S TO THE HEALTH OF MARRIED WOMEN!
AND A SMILE LURKS AT THE CORNER OF MY MOUTH
HERE'S TO THE HEALTH OF MARRIED WOMEN, AND
    THEIR LOVERS!

DOLOKHOV & CHORUS.
HERE'S TO THE HEALTH OF MARRIED WOMEN!

> HERE'S TO THE HEALTH OF MARRIED WOMEN, AND
> THEIR LOVERS!
> HERE'S TO THE HEALTH OF MARRIED WOMEN!
> HERE'S TO THE HEALTH OF MARRIED WOMEN, AND
> THEIR LOVERS!

PIERRE.
> HOW DARE YOU TOUCH HER?

DOLOKHOV.
> YOU CAN'T LOVE HER

PIERRE.
> ENOUGH!
> YOU BULLY, YOU SCOUNDREL!
> I CHALLENGE YOU!

DOLOKHOV.
> OH, A DUEL!
> YES, THIS IS WHAT I LIKE

HÉLÈNE.
> HE WILL KILL YOU!
> STUPID HUSBAND!

PIERRE.
> SO I SHALL BE KILLED!
> WHAT IS IT TO YOU!
> ANATOLE, MY GUNS

ANATOLE.
> OH! THIS IS HORRIBLY STUPID

DOLOKHOV.
> WELL LET'S BEGIN!
> THIS IS CHILD'S PLAY

SERVANT (DENISOV).
> AS THE ADVERSARIES HAVE REFUSED A RECONCILIATION,
> WE SHALL PLEASE PROCEED WITH THE DUEL
> READY YOUR PISTOLS, AND ON THE COUNT OF TRI, BEGIN
> TO ADVANCE

ALL.
> *RAZ! DVA! TRI!*

>> (**PIERRE** *and* **DOLOKHOV** *start toward each other.*)

ANATOLE.
>PIERRE, HOLD YOUR FIRE
>PIERRE, HOLD YOUR FIRE
>PIERRE, NOT YET!

>>(**PIERRE** *fires early;* **DOLOKHOV** *is hit.*)

DOLOKHOV.
>NO!...
>SHOT BY A FOOL

PIERRE.
>NO WAIT –
>I DIDN'T –

DOLOKHOV.
>QUIET OLD MAN
>MY TURN

PIERRE.
>MY TURN

ANATOLE.
>PIERRE, STAND BACK!

>>(**PIERRE** *walks toward* **DOLOKHOV** *with his chest exposed.* **DOLOKHOV** *shoots.* **PIERRE** *is unharmed.*)

DOLOKHOV.
>MISSED
>MISSED
>OH MY MOTHER, MY ANGEL
>MY ADORED ANGEL MOTHER!

HÉLÈNE.
>TAKE HIM AWAY

SERVANT (DENISOV).
>THE SUN IS RISING
>THE DUEL IS AT AN END
>AND PIERRE BEZUKHOV IS THE WINNER

PIERRE.
>WINNER?

HÉLÈNE.
>YOU ARE A FOOL

*(Two **CLUBGOERS** laugh at **PIERRE** as they leave.)*

ANATOLE.
>WELL SWEET SISTER
>YOU CERTAINLY BRING OUT THE BEAST IN MEN

HÉLÈNE.
>WHAT CAN I SAY?
>IT'S A GIFT

ANATOLE.
>HOW I ADORE YOU
>WILL YOU ASK NATASHA TO THE BALL TONIGHT?

HÉLÈNE.
>OF COURSE
>DEAR BROTHER

>>*(She leaves. **ANATOLE** turns to **PIERRE**.)*

ANATOLE.
>COME ON OLD MAN
>LET'S GET YOU HOME

PIERRE.
>IN A MOMENT

ANATOLE.
>SLEEP IT OFF
>AND BE HAPPY
>WE LIVE TO LOVE ANOTHER DAY

10. "DUST AND ASHES"

PIERRE.
>IS THIS HOW I DIE?
>RIDICULED AND LAUGHED AT
>WEARING CLOWN SHOES
>IS THIS HOW I DIE?
>FURIOUS AND RECKLESS
>SICK WITH BOOZE
>
>HOW DID I LIVE?
>I TASTE EVERY WASTED MINUTE
>EVERY TIME I TURNED AWAY
>FROM THE THINGS THAT MIGHT HAVE HEALED ME
>HOW LONG HAVE I BEEN SLEEPING?
>
>IS THIS HOW I DIE?
>FRIGHTENED LIKE A CHILD
>LAZY AND NUMB
>IS THIS HOW I DIE?
>PRETENDING AND PREPOSTEROUS
>AND DUMB
>
>HOW DID I LIVE?
>WAS I KIND ENOUGH AND GOOD ENOUGH?
>DID I LOVE ENOUGH?
>DID I EVER LOOK UP
>AND SEE THE MOON
>AND THE STARS
>AND THE SKY?
>OH WHY HAVE I BEEN SLEEPING?
>
>THEY SAY WE ARE ASLEEP
>UNTIL WE FALL IN LOVE
>WE ARE CHILDREN OF DUST AND ASHES
>BUT WHEN WE FALL IN LOVE WE WAKE UP
>AND WE ARE A GOD
>AND ANGELS WEEP
>BUT IF I DIE HERE TONIGHT
>I DIE IN MY SLEEP
>
>ALL OF MY LIFE I SPENT SEARCHING THE WORDS

OF POETS AND SAINTS AND PROPHETS AND KINGS
AND NOW AT THE END ALL I KNOW THAT I'VE LEARNED
IS THAT ALL THAT I KNOW IS I DON'T KNOW A THING

SO EASY TO CLOSE OFF
PLACE THE BLAME OUTSIDE
HIDING IN MY ROOM AT NIGHT
SO TERRIFIED

ALL THE THINGS I COULD HAVE BEEN
BUT I NEVER HAD THE NERVE
LIFE AND LOVE
I DON'T DESERVE

SO ALL RIGHT, ALL RIGHT
I'VE HAD MY TIME
CLOSE MY EYES
LET THE DEATH BELLS CHIME

BURY ME IN BURGUNDY
I JUST DON'T CARE
NOTHING'S LEFT
I LOOKED EVERYWHERE

IS THIS HOW I DIE?
WAS THERE EVER ANY OTHER WAY MY LIFE COULD BE?
IS THIS HOW I DIE?
SUCH A STORM OF FEELINGS INSIDE OF ME

BUT THEN WHY AM I SCREAMING?
WHY AM I SHAKING?
OH GOD, WAS THERE SOMETHING THAT I MISSED?
DID I SQUANDER MY DIVINITY?
WAS HAPPINESS WITHIN ME THE WHOLE TIME?

THEY SAY WE ARE ASLEEP
UNTIL WE FALL IN LOVE
WE ARE CHILDREN OF DUST AND ASHES
BUT WHEN WE FALL IN LOVE WE WAKE UP
AND WE ARE A GOD
AND ANGELS WEEP
BUT IF I DIE HERE TONIGHT
I DIE IN MY SLEEP

THEY SAY WE ARE ASLEEP
UNTIL WE FALL IN LOVE
AND I'M SO READY
TO WAKE UP NOW

I WANT TO WAKE UP
DON'T LET ME DIE WHILE I'M LIKE THIS
I WANT TO WAKE UP
GOD DON'T LET ME DIE WHILE I'M LIKE THIS
PLEASE LET ME WAKE UP NOW
GOD DON'T LET ME DIE WHILE I'M LIKE THIS
I'M READY
I'M READY
TO WAKE UP

Chapter 5

11. "SUNDAY MORNING"

SONYA.
>EARLY SUNDAY MORNING
>NATASHA AND I LIT A CANDLE
>LOOKED IN THE MIRROR

NATASHA.
>I SEE MY FACE

SONYA.
>DON'T BE SILLY
>
>THEY SAY YOU CAN SEE YOUR FUTURE
>IN THE LONG ROW OF CANDLES
>STRETCHING BACK AND BACK AND BACK
>INTO THE DEPTHS OF THE MIRROR
>IN THE DIM CONFUSED LAST SQUARE
>YOU'LL SEE A COFFIN OR A MAN
>EVERYONE SEES A MAN

NATASHA.
>I SEE THE CANDLES
>STRETCHING BACK
>SO FAR AWAY
>I SEE THE MIRRORS
>I SEE A SHAPE IN THE DARKNESS
>IS IT HIM OR IS IT –
>HE'S LYING DOWN
>OH SONYA WHY IS HE LYING DOWN?
>I'M SO FRIGHTENED!
>ANDREY WILL NEVER COME
>OR SOMETHING WILL HAPPEN TO ME BEFORE HE DOES

MARYA D.
>SUNDAY MORNING!
>TIME FOR CHURCH!

NATASHA.
>I SUFFER MORE NOW THAN BEFORE

THE THEATER AND ANATOLE
THAT MAN WHO AROUSED SUCH TERRIBLE FEELINGS
I DON'T UNDERSTAND
HAVE I BROKEN FAITH WITH ANDREY?
AM I GUILTY?

SONYA.

AFTER CHURCH, MARYA LEFT FOR PRINCE BOLKONSKY'S

MARYA D.

THE RUDENESS OF THAT MAN!
I'LL STRAIGHTEN HIM OUT!

NATASHA.

THAT TERRIBLE OLD PRINCE
I CAN'T BEAR TO THINK OF IT
I'LL SHUT MYSELF IN MY ROOM
AND TRY ON NEW DRESSES

SONYA.

AND JUST AFTER MARYA LEFT
THERE WAS A KNOCK AT THE DOOR
NATASHA HAD JUST TURNED HER HEAD TO THE GLASS
WHEN SHE HEARD A VOICE THAT MADE HER FLUSH

12. "CHARMING"

HÉLÈNE.
    OH MY ENCHANTRESS
    OH YOU BEAUTIFUL THING
    CHARMING, CHARMING
    OH, THIS IS REALLY BEYOND ANYTHING
    THESE DRESSES SUIT YOU
    THIS ONE, "METALLIC GAUZE"
    STRAIGHT FROM PARIS

    ANYTHING SUITS YOU, MY CHARMER
    OH HOW SHE BLUSHES, HOW SHE BLUSHES, MY PRETTY!
    OH HOW SHE BLUSHES, HOW SHE BLUSHES, MY PRETTY!
    CHARMANTE, CHARMANTE!
    YOU ARE SUCH A LOVELY THING
    OH WHERE HAVE YOU BEEN?
    IT'S SUCH A SHAME TO BURY PEARLS IN THE COUNTRY
    CHARMANTE, CHARMANTE, CHARMING

    NOW IF YOU HAVE A DRESS
    YOU MUST WEAR IT OUT
    HOW CAN YOU LIVE IN MOSCOW AND NOT GO NOWHERE?
    SO YOU LOVE SOMEBODY, CHARMING
    BUT THAT'S NO REASON TO SHUT YOURSELF IN
    EVEN IF YOU'RE ENGAGED
    YOU MUST WEAR YOUR DRESS OUT SOMEWHERE

    MY BROTHER DINED WITH ME YESTERDAY
    BUT HE DIDN'T EAT A THING
    CUZ HE WAS THINKING 'BOUT YOU
    HE KEPT SIGHING ABOUT YOU

    OH HOW SHE BLUSHES, HOW SHE BLUSHES, MY PRETTY!
    OH HOW SHE BLUSHES, HOW SHE BLUSHES, MY PRETTY!
    CHARMANTE, CHARMANTE!
    YOU ARE SUCH A LOVELY THING
    OH WHERE HAVE YOU BEEN?
    IT'S SUCH A SHAME TO BURY PEARLS IN THE COUNTRY
    CHARMANTE, CHARMANTE, CHARMING

    NOW A WOMAN WITH A DRESS

IS A FRIGHTENING AND POWERFUL THING
YOU ARE NOT A CHILD
WHEN YOU'RE DRAPED IN SCARLET AND LACE
YOUR FIANCÉ WOULD WANT YOU TO HAVE FUN
RATHER THAN BE BORED TO DEATH
ALLIEZ DANS LE MONDE
PLUTÔT QUE DE DÉPÉRIR D'ENNUI!

MY BROTHER IS QUITE MADLY IN LOVE
HE IS QUITE MADLY IN LOVE WITH YOU, MY DEAR

OH HOW SHE BLUSHES, HOW SHE BLUSHES, MY PRETTY!
OH HOW SHE BLUSHES, HOW SHE BLUSHES, MY PRETTY!
CHARMANTE, CHARMANTE!
YOU ARE SUCH A LOVELY THING
OH WHERE HAVE YOU BEEN?
IT'S SUCH A SHAME TO BURY PEARLS IN THE COUNTRY
CHARMANTE, CHARMANTE, CHARMING
SUCH A SHAME TO BURY PEARLS IN THE COUNTRY
CHARMANTE, CHARMANTE, CHARMING

NATASHA.
WHAT ONCE SEEMED SO TERRIBLE
NOW SEEMS SIMPLE AND NATURAL
SHE KNOWS THAT I'M ENGAGED
AND STILL SHE TALKS SO FRANKLY
SO IT MUST BE ALL RIGHT!

HÉLÈNE.
THERE IS A BALL AT MY HOUSE TONIGHT
YOU MUST COME
OH YOUR WIDE-OPEN, WONDERING EYES!
YOU WILL BE THE PRETTIEST THERE!
HOW THE THOUGHT OF THROWING THEM TOGETHER
 AMUSES ME!
YOU MUST COME

NATASHA.
I WILL COME

Chapter 6

13. "THE BALL"

ANATOLE.
> WAITING AT THE DOOR
> WAITING AT THE DOOR
> WAITING
>
> WAITING AT THE DOOR
> WAITING AT THE DOOR
> WAITING
> HOW I ADORE LITTLE GIRLS
> THEY LOSE THEIR HEADS AT ONCE
>> *(The ball begins;* **ANATOLE** *and* **NATASHA** *dance.)*

NATASHA.
> I AM SEIZED BY FEELINGS OF VANITY AND FEAR
> THERE IS NO BARRIER BETWEEN US
> WHISPERS AND MOANS AND RINGING IN MY EAR
> THERE IS NO BARRIER BETWEEN US
>
> DIVINE, DELICIOUS
> BUT I DO NOT SEE OR HEAR ANYTHING
> I'M BORNE AWAY TO A SENSELESS WORLD
> SO STRANGE, SO REMOTE
> I DON'T KNOW GOOD FROM BAD
> ANATOLE
> ANATOLE
> I'M SO FRIGHTENED

ANATOLE.
> YOU ARE ENCHANTING

NATASHA.
> AND AS WE DANCED HE PRESSED MY WAIST AND HAND
> AND TOLD ME I WAS

NATASHA & ANATOLE.
> BEWITCHING

ANATOLE.
>AND I LOVE YOU

NATASHA & ANATOLE.
>BEWITCHING

ANATOLE.
>AND I LOVE YOU

NATASHA.
>AND DURING THE ECOSSAISE, HE

NATASHA (& ANATOLE).
>GAZED/(GAZE) IN MY EYES

NATASHA.
>AND SAID NOTHING, JUST

NATASHA (& ANATOLE).
>GAZED/(GAZE) IN MY EYES

NATASHA.
>MY FRIGHTENED EYES
>
>SUCH CONFIDENT TENDERNESS
>I COULD NOT SAY WHAT I HAD TO SAY

ANATOLE.
>DON'T LOWER YOUR EYES
>I LOVE YOU
>I AM IN LOVE DEAR
>I AM IN LOVE
>
>GAZE IN MY EYES
>I LOVE YOU
>YOU ARE BEWITCHING
>WHAT CAN I DO?
>DARLING WHAT CAN I DO?

NATASHA.
>DON'T SAY SUCH THINGS
>I AM BETROTHED
>I LOVE ANOTHER

ANATOLE.
>DON'T SPEAK TO ME OF THAT!
>WHEN I TELL YOU THAT I AM MADLY, MADLY IN LOVE
>>WITH YOU!

IS IT MY FAULT THAT YOU'RE ENCHANTING?
NATASHA.
> I'M SO FRIGHTENED
> I DON'T UNDERSTAND ANYTHING TONIGHT

ANATOLE.
> I'M HERE NOW

>> (**NATASHA** *breaks away.*)

> NATALIE!

NATASHA.
> I CAN FEEL YOUR EYES UPON ME

ANATOLE.
> BLOCKING HER PATH, I BRING HER FACE CLOSE TO MINE

NATASHA.
> HIS LARGE, GLITTERING, MASCULINE EYES ARE SO CLOSE TO MINE
> THAT I SEE NOTHING ELSE

ANATOLE.
> IS IT POSSIBLE THAT I SHOULD NEVER SEE YOU AGAIN?
> I LOVE YOU MADLY!
> CAN I NEVER?
> NATALIE?

NATASHA.
> YOU PRESS MY ARM

ANATOLE.
> NATALIE?

NATASHA.
> YOU'RE HURTING MY HANDS

ANATOLE.
> NATALIE?

NATASHA.
> I DON'T UNDERSTAND
> I HAVE NOTHING TO SAY

>> *(They kiss.)*

> BURNING LIPS PRESSED TO MINE
> TELL ME WHAT JUST HAPPENED

I'M TREMBLING
SO FRIGHTENING

ANDREY

BUT I LOVE YOU
OF THAT THERE IS NO DOUBT
HOW ELSE COULD ALL OF THIS HAVE HAPPENED?
HOW ELSE COULD WE HAVE KISSED?
IT MEANS THAT I HAVE LOVED YOU FROM THE FIRST
IT MEANS THAT YOU ARE KIND, NOBLE, AND SPLENDID
AND I COULD NOT HELP LOVING YOU

I WILL LOVE YOU ANATOLE
I'LL DO ANYTHING FOR YOU

NATASHA & ANATOLE.

I'LL DO ANYTHING FOR YOU

PART IV

Chapter 7

14. "LETTERS"

ALL.
>IN NINETEENTH CENTURY RUSSIA WE WRITE LETTERS
>WE WRITE LETTERS
>WE PUT DOWN IN WRITING
>WHAT IS HAPPENING IN OUR MINDS
>
>ONCE IT'S ON THE PAPER WE FEEL BETTER
>WE FEEL BETTER
>IT'S LIKE SOME KIND OF CLARITY
>WHEN THE LETTER'S DONE AND SIGNED

PIERRE.
>DEAR ANDREY
>DEAR OLD FRIEND
>HOW GOES THE WAR?
>DO WE MARCH ON THE FRENCH SPLENDIDLY?
>DO OUR CANNONS CRACK AND CRY?
>DO OUR BULLETS WHISTLE AND SING?
>DOES THE AIR REEK WITH SMOKE?
>
>I WISH I WERE THERE
>WITH DEATH AT MY HEELS
>
>DOLOKHOV IS RECOVERING
>HE WILL BE ALL RIGHT THE GOOD MAN
>AND NATASHA IS IN TOWN
>YOUR BRIDE-TO-BE, SO FULL OF LIFE AND MISCHIEF
>I SHOULD VISIT
>I HEAR SHE IS MORE BEAUTIFUL THAN EVER

HOW I ENVY YOU AND YOUR HAPPINESS

HERE AT HOME
I DRINK AND READ AND DRINK AND READ AND DRINK
BUT I THINK I FINALLY FOUND IT
WHAT MY HEART HAS NEEDED

FOR I'VE BEEN STUDYING THE KABAL
AND I'VE CALCULATED THE NUMBER OF THE BEAST
IT IS NAPOLEON
SIX HUNDRED THREE SCORE AND SIX
AND I WILL KILL HIM ONE DAY
HE'S NO GREAT MAN
NONE OF US ARE GREAT MEN
WE'RE CAUGHT IN THE WAVE OF HISTORY
NOTHING MATTERS
EVERYTHING MATTERS
IT'S ALL THE SAME
OH IF ONLY I COULD NOT SEE IT
THIS DREADFUL, TERRIBLE *IT*!

ALL.

IN NINETEENTH CENTURY RUSSIA WE WRITE LETTERS
WE WRITE LETTERS

NATASHA & PIERRE.

WE WRITE LETTERS

ALL.

WE PUT DOWN IN WRITING
WHAT IS HAPPENING IN OUR MINDS

NATASHA.

DEAR ANDREY –

WHAT MORE CAN I WRITE
AFTER ALL THAT HAS HAPPENED?
WHAT AM I TO DO IF I LOVE HIM AND THE OTHER ONE TOO?
MUST I BREAK IT OFF?
THESE TERRIBLE QUESTIONS

NATASHA & PIERRE.

I SEE NOTHING BUT THE CANDLE IN THE MIRROR
NO VISIONS OF THE FUTURE

SO LOST AND ALONE

NATASHA.

AND WHAT OF PRINCESS MARY –

MARY.

DEAR NATASHA
I'M IN DEEP DESPAIR AT THE MISUNDERSTANDING THERE
    IS BETWEEN US
WHATEVER MY FATHER'S FEELINGS MIGHT BE
I BEG YOU TO BELIEVE THAT I CANNOT HELP LOVING YOU
HE IS A TIRED OLD MAN AND MUST BE FORGIVEN
PLEASE, COME SEE US AGAIN

NATASHA.

DEAR PRINCESS MARY –

OH WHAT AM I TO WRITE?!
HOW DO I CHOOSE?
WHAT DO I DO?
I SHALL NEVER BE HAPPY AGAIN

PIERRE.

THESE TERRIBLE QUESTIONS

MARY.

I'M SO ALONE HERE

NATASHA & PIERRE.

SO ALONE IN HERE

MARY.

AND I SEE NOTHING

NATASHA, PIERRE & MARY.

I SEE NOTHING BUT THE CANDLE IN THE MIRROR
NO VISIONS OF THE FUTURE
SO LOST AND ALONE

ALL.

IN NINETEENTH CENTURY RUSSIA WE WRITE LETTERS
WE WRITE LETTERS

NATASHA & PIERRE.

WE WRITE LETTERS

MARY & ANATOLE.

WE WRITE LETTERS

ALL.
> WE PUT DOWN IN WRITING
> WHAT IS HAPPENING IN OUR MINDS

ANATOLE.
> DEAR NATALIE
> A LOVE LETTER
> A LOVE LETTER
> A LOVE LETTER

NATASHA.
> A LETTER FROM HIM, FROM THE MAN THAT I LOVE

DOLOKHOV.
> A LETTER WHICH I COMPOSED

ALL.
> A LOVE LETTER
> A LOVE LETTER…

ANATOLE.
> NATALIE NATALIE NATALIE
> I MUST LOVE YOU OR DIE
> NATALIE NATALIE NATALIE
> IF YOU LOVE ME SAY YES
> AND I WILL COME AND STEAL YOU AWAY
> STEAL YOU OUT OF THE DARK
> NATALIE NATALIE NATALIE
> I WANT NOTHING MORE
>
> NATALIE NATALIE NATALIE
> I MUST LOVE YOU OR DIE
> NATALIE NATALIE NATALIE
> IF YOU LOVE ME SAY YES
> AND I WILL COME AND STEAL YOU AWAY
> STEAL YOU OUT OF THE DARK
> NATALIE NATALIE NATALIE
> I WANT NOTHING MORE
>
> JUST SAY YES
> JUST SAY YES
> JUST SAY YES

NATASHA.
> YES, YES, I LOVE HIM!

HOW ELSE COULD I HAVE HIS LETTER IN MY HAND?
I READ IT TWENTY TIMES
THIRTY TIMES, FORTY TIMES!
EACH AND EVERY WORD
I LOVE HIM, I LOVE HIM

> (**NATASHA** *sleeps.* **SONYA** *arrives and reads Anatole's letter.*)

Chapter 8

15. "SONYA & NATASHA"

SONYA.
>HOW WAS IT I NOTICED NOTHING?
>HOW COULD IT GO SO FAR?
>IT CAN'T BE THAT SHE LOVES HIM
>IT CAN'T BE
>NATASHA

>>(**NATASHA** *awakes and sees* **SONYA**.)

NATASHA.
>SONYA, YOU'RE BACK
>AND WITH THE TENDER RESOLVE THAT OFTEN COMES AT
>>THE MOMENT OF AWAKENING
>
>I EMBRACED MY FRIEND
>BUT NOTICING SONYA'S LOOK OF EMBARRASSMENT
>MY FACE EXPRESSED CONFUSION
>AND SUSPICION
>
>SONYA, YOU'VE READ THE LETTER?

SONYA.
>YES

NATASHA.
>OH SONYA, I'M GLAD
>I CAN'T HIDE IT ANY LONGER!
>NOW YOU KNOW, WE LOVE ONE ANOTHER!
>OH SONYA, HE WRITES, HE WRITES
>HE WRITES, HE WRITES, HE WRITES

SONYA.
>AND ANDREY?

NATASHA.
>OH SONYA, IF YOU ONLY KNEW HOW HAPPY I AM!
>YOU DON'T KNOW WHAT LOVE IS

SONYA.
>BUT NATASHA, CAN THAT ALL BE OVER?

NATASHA.

I DO NOT GRASP THE QUESTION

SONYA.

ARE YOU REFUSING PRINCE ANDREY?

NATASHA.

OH, YOU DON'T UNDERSTAND ANYTHING!
DON'T TALK NONSENSE, JUST LISTEN

SONYA.

BUT I CAN'T BELIEVE IT, I DON'T UNDERSTAND
HOW YOU LOVED ONE MAN A WHOLE YEAR
AND SUDDENLY –
YOU'VE ONLY KNOWN HIM THREE DAYS!
NATASHA, YOU'RE JOKING!

NATASHA.

THREE DAYS?
IT SEEMS TO ME I'VE LOVED HIM A HUNDRED YEARS
IT SEEMS TO ME I'VE NEVER LOVED ANYONE BEFORE
NOT LIKE THIS
I HAVE NO WILL
MY LIFE IS HIS
I'LL DO ANYTHING HE WANTS ME TO
WHAT CAN I DO?
SONYA, WHAT CAN I DO?

I'M SO HAPPY
AND SO FRIGHTENED
WHY CAN'T YOU UNDERSTAND?
I LOVE HIM!

SONYA.

THEN I WON'T LET IT COME TO THAT, I SHALL TELL!
BURSTING INTO TEARS

NATASHA.

WHAT DO YOU MEAN?
FOR GOD'S SAKE, IF YOU TELL, YOU ARE MY ENEMY!
YOU WANT ME TO BE MISERABLE
YOU WANT TO TEAR US APART
FOR GOD'S SAKE, SONYA, DON'T TELL ANYONE, DON'T
  TORTURE ME

I HAVE CONFIDED IN YOU

SONYA.

WHAT HAS HAPPENED BETWEEN YOU?
WHAT HAS HE SAID TO YOU?
WHY DOESN'T HE COME TO THE HOUSE AND OPENLY ASK
 FOR YOUR HAND?
WHY THIS SECRECY?
HAVE YOU THOUGHT WHAT HIS SECRET REASONS MAY
 BE?

NATASHA.

I DON'T KNOW WHAT THE REASONS ARE
BUT THERE MUST BE REASONS!
SONYA, ONE CAN'T DOUBT HIM!

SONYA.

DOES HE LOVE YOU?

NATASHA.

DOES HE LOVE ME?
WHY, YOU'VE READ HIS LETTER, YOU'VE SEEN HIM
I CAN'T LIVE WITHOUT HIM

SONYA.

NATASHA, THINK OF OUR FAMILY
AND THINK OF PRINCE ANDREY

NATASHA.

ANDREY SAID I WAS FREE TO REFUSE HIM

SONYA.

BUT YOU HAVEN'T REFUSED HIM, OR HAVE YOU?

NATASHA.

PERHAPS I HAVE
PERHAPS ALL IS OVER BETWEEN ME AND BOLKONSKY
WOULD YOU THINK SO BADLY OF ME?

SONYA.

I WON'T SUCCUMB TO YOUR TENDER TONE NATASHA
I DON'T TRUST HIM, NATASHA!
I'M AFRAID FOR YOU, NATASHA!
AFRAID YOU ARE GOING TO YOUR RUIN

NATASHA.

THEN I'LL GO TO MY RUIN, YES I WILL, AS SOON AS
 POSSIBLE!

BUT IT'S NOT YOUR BUSINESS!
IT WON'T BE YOU, IT'LL BE ME, WHO'LL SUFFER
LEAVE ME ALONE, YES LEAVE ME ALONE!
I HATE YOU SONYA!
I HATE YOU SONYA!
I HATE YOU, I HATE YOU!
YOU'RE MY ENEMY FOREVER!

SONYA.

I BURST INTO SOBS

(**NATASHA** *runs out of the room.*)

NATASHA.

AND WITHOUT A MOMENT'S REFLECTION
I WROTE THE ANSWER TO PRINCESS MARY
I'D BEEN UNABLE TO WRITE ALL MORNING

ALL OUR MISUNDERSTANDINGS ARE AT AN END;
FORGET EVERYTHING AND FORGIVE ME
BUT I CAN'T BE ANDREY'S WIFE

16. "SONYA ALONE"

SONYA.
>HARD AS IT IS
>IN THE COMING DAYS
>I WATCH MY FRIEND
>IN HER STRANGE UNNATURAL STATE
>DON'T LET HER OUT OF MY SIGHT
>SHE TRAILS OFF
>STARES AT NOTHING
>LAUGHS AT RANDOM
>AND THE LETTERS COME
>
>SHE WAITS BY THE WINDOW
>AND I LISTEN AT THE DOOR
>
>UNTIL ONE DAY
>I SEE BY THE SAD LOOK ON HER FACE
>THERE IS A DREADFUL PLAN IN HER HEART
>
>I KNOW YOU ARE CAPABLE OF ANYTHING
>I KNOW YOU SO WELL MY FRIEND
>I KNOW YOU MIGHT JUST RUN AWAY
>WHAT AM I TO DO?
>WHO DO I ASK FOR HELP?
>IS IT ALL ON ME?
>IS IT ALL ON ME?
>
>I WILL STAND IN THE DARK FOR YOU
>I WILL HOLD YOU BACK BY FORCE
>I WILL STAND HERE RIGHT OUTSIDE YOUR DOOR
>I WON'T SEE YOU DISGRACED
>I WILL PROTECT YOUR NAME AND YOUR HEART
>BECAUSE I MISS MY FRIEND
>
>I KNOW YOU'VE FORGOTTEN ME
>I KNOW YOU SO WELL MY FRIEND
>I KNOW YOU MIGHT JUST THROW YOURSELF OVER
>BUT I WON'T LET YOU
>I WON'T LET YOU
>IT'S ALL ON ME

AND I REMEMBER THIS FAMILY
I REMEMBER THEIR KINDNESS
AND IF I NEVER SLEEP AGAIN

I WILL STAND IN THE DARK FOR YOU
I WILL HOLD YOU BACK BY FORCE
I WILL STAND HERE RIGHT OUTSIDE YOUR DOOR
I WON'T SEE YOU DISGRACED
I WILL PROTECT YOUR NAME AND YOUR HEART
BECAUSE I MISS MY FRIEND
BECAUSE I MISS MY FRIEND
BECAUSE I MISS YOU, MY FRIEND

Chapter 9

17. "PREPARATIONS"

(**PIERRE** *runs into* **ANATOLE** *on the street.* **PIERRE** *is drunk,* **ANATOLE** *in a hurry.*)

PIERRE.

AH, ANATOLE! WHERE ARE YOU OFF TO?

ANATOLE.

PIERRE, GOOD MAN
TONIGHT I GO AWAY, ON AN ADVENTURE
YOU'LL NOT BE SEEING ME FOR SOME TIME
I'VE FOUND A NEW PLEASURE
AND I'M TAKING HER AWAY
I'LL SEND YOU A LETTER FROM POLAND

PIERRE.

HA! AN ELOPEMENT!
FOOL, YOU ARE MARRIED ALREADY!

ANATOLE.

DON'T TALK TO ME OF THAT!
I WILL NOT DEPRIVE MYSELF OF THIS ONE!
TONIGHT! I TAKE HER TONIGHT!
LEND ME FIFTY RUBLES?

PIERRE.

AH, THAT'S A TRUE SAGE
LIVING IN THE MOMENT
WHAT I WOULDN'T GIVE TO BE LIKE HIM

DOLOKHOV.

THE PLAN FOR NATALIE ROSTOVA'S ABDUCTION
HAD ALL BEEN ARRANGED AND THE PREPARATIONS MADE
ON THE DAY THAT SONYA DECIDED TO SAVE HER
THAT WAS THE DAY THAT THE GAME WAS TO BE PLAYED
NATASHA WAS TO BE ON HER BACK PORCH AT TEN
ANATOLE AND HIS TROIKA WOULD SCOOP HER UP AND THEN

THEY'D RIDE FORTY MILES TO THE VILLAGE OF KAMENKA
WHERE AN UNFROCKED PRIEST WAS TO MAKE 'EM GET WED
THEN BACK INTO THE TROIKA OFF THEY'D GO
TAKE THE POLAND HIGHROAD TO THE WEDDING BED

ANATOLE.
PASSPORTS, HORSES, TEN THOUSAND RUBLES I HAVE TAKEN FROM MY SISTER
AND ANOTHER TEN THOUSAND RAISED WITH DOLOKHOV'S HELP

DOLOKHOV.
WE WERE GATHERED IN MY STUDY DRINKING UP SOME TEA
JUST ANATOLE THE TWO WEDDING WITNESSES AND ME
AN ABACUS AND PAPER MONEY STREWN ON THE DESK
PERSIAN RUGS AND BEARSKINS HANGING GROTESQUE
ANATOLE WAS WALKING WITH HIS UNIFORM UNBUTTONED
WALKING TO AND FRO
TO AND FRO
TO AND FRO

ANATOLE & DOLOKHOV.
TO AND FRO
TO AND FRO
TO AND FRO
TO AND FRO

DOLOKHOV.
NOW WAIT!
YOU BETTER
JUST
GIVE IT UP NOW
WHY DONTCHA
WHILE THERE'S STILL TIME!
YOU'D REALLY BETTER DROP IT ALL
GIVE IT UP NOW!
WHILE THERE'S STILL TIME!
DO YOU KNOW?

ANATOLE.
> WHAT, TEASING AGAIN?
> FOOL DON'T TALK NONSENSE!
> GO TO THE DEVIL EH?
> REALLY THIS IS NO TIME FOR YOUR STUPID JOKES

DOLOKHOV.
> I AM NOT JOKING, I AM TALKING SENSE
> THIS IS SERIOUS BUSINESS, A DANGEROUS BUSINESS
> COME HERE, COME HERE, COME HERE ANATOLE!
> WHY WOULD I JOKE ABOUT IT?
> ME OF ALL PEOPLE
> WHO FOUND THE PRIEST, RAISED THE MONEY, GOT THE PASSPORTS, GOT THE HORSES?

ANATOLE.
> AND WELL I THANK YOU FOR IT
> DO YOU THINK I AM NOT GRATEFUL?

DOLOKHOV.
> AND NOW YOU'LL CARRY HER AWAY BUT WILL THEY LET IT STOP THERE?
> YOU HAVEN'T THOUGHT THIS THROUGH OR DO YOU JUST DON'T CARE?
> NOW LISTEN TO ME TELL IT TO YOU ONE LAST TIME
> THEY WILL TAKE YOU TO THE COURT AND CONVICT YOU FOR YOUR CRIME
> ALREADY MARRIED AND YOU'RE PLAYING WITH A LITTLE GIRL
> DON'T YOU KNOW, DON'T YOU THINK, DON'T YOU KNOW?

ANATOLE.
> NONSENSE, NONSENSE!
> I'M SCOWLING AND GRIMACING
> DIDN'T I EXPLAIN IT TO YOU, DIDN'T I, WHAT?

DOLOKHOV.
> AND HERE ANATOLE
> WITH THE STUBBORN ATTACHMENT SMALL-MINDED PEOPLE HAVE
> FOR CONCLUSIONS THEY'VE WORKED OUT FOR THEMSELVES

REPEATED HIS ARGUMENT TO ME FOR THE HUNDREDTH TIME

ANATOLE.
IF THIS MARRIAGE ISN'T VALID
THEN I'M OFF THE HOOK
BUT IF IT IS VALID, IT REALLY DOESN'T MATTER!
NO ONE ABROAD IS GONNA KNOW A THING ABOUT IT
ISN'T THAT SO NOW DON'T YOU KNOW,
DON'T TALK TO ME, DON'T DON'T WHAT WHAT
AH GO TO HELL NOW
I'M CLUTCHING MY HAIR!
IT'S THE VERY DEVIL!
HERE, FEEL HOW IT BEATS!

*(He presses **DOLOKHOV**'s hand to his heart. A light comes up on **NATASHA** across the room.)*

AH MA CHERE, MA CHERE
QUEL PIED, QUEL REGARD!
WHAT A FOOT SHE HAS, WHAT A GLANCE,
A GODDESS!

AND MY HANDSOME LIPS
MUTTER SOMETHING TENDER TO MYSELF

IT'S TIME!
IT'S TIME!
NOW THEN! NEARLY READY? YOU'RE DAWDLING!
THE DRIVER IS HERE
THE DRIVER IS HERE
BALAGA IS HERE!

18. "BALAGA"

ANATOLE & DOLOKHOV.
>HEY BALAGA
>HO BALAGA
>HEY HEY HO BALAGA
>HEY HEY BALAGA
>THE FAMOUS TROIKA DRIVER
>
>HEY BALAGA
>HO BALAGA
>HEY HEY HEY BALAGA
>HEY HEY BALAGA
>THE FAMOUS TROIKA DRIVER

BALAGA.
>WHO'S THAT MADMAN FLYING AT FULL GALLOP DOWN
>   THE STREET?
>WHO'S THAT MADMAN KNOCKING PEOPLE OVER
>RUNNING PEOPLE DOWN
>WHILE HIS FINE GENTLEMEN
>HOLD ON TO THEIR SEATS?

ANATOLE & DOLOKHOV.
>IT'S BALAGA!

BALAGA.
>DRIVING MAD AT TWELVE MILES AN HOUR

ANATOLE & DOLOKHOV.
>BALAGA!

BALAGA.
>COMIN' STRAIGHT AT YOU
>GET OUT MY WAY, GET OUT MY WAY

ANATOLE & DOLOKHOV.
>BALAGA!

BALAGA.
>LASHIN' MY WHIP AT HORSES AND PEASANTS

ANATOLE & DOLOKHOV.
>BALAGA!

BALAGA.
>RISKING SKIN AND LIFE TWENTY TIMES A YEAR

FOR MY FINE FINE GENTLEMEN
YESSIR HEY HO YESSIR
YESSIR YESSIR YESSIR

ANATOLE & DOLOKHOV.
MORE THAN ONCE!

BALAGA.
FROM TULA TO MOSCOW AND BACK IN JUST ONE NIGHT

ANATOLE & DOLOKHOV.
MORE THAN ONCE!

BALAGA.
A NARROW ESCAPE FROM A WILD COSSACK FIGHT

ANATOLE & DOLOKHOV.
MORE THAN ONCE!

BALAGA.
THEY'VE BEATEN ME AND SLAPPED ME WITH THEIR
  GLOVES

ANATOLE & DOLOKHOV.
MORE THAN ONCE!

BALAGA.
MADE ME DRUNK ON CHAMPAGNE, WHICH I LOVE!

ALL.
HEY BALAGA
HO BALAGA
HEY HEY HO BALAGA
HEY HEY BALAGA
THE FAMOUS TROIKA DRIVER

HEY BALAGA
HO BALAGA
HEY HEY HEY BALAGA
HEY HEY BALAGA
THE FAMOUS TROIKA DRIVER

ANATOLE.
WHO'S THAT SLOWPOKE WE ABUSE WITH WILD AND
  TIPSY SHOUTS?

BALAGA.
WHO KNOWS THINGS THAT WOULD GET YOU SENT
  STRAIGHT TO SIBERIA

IF ANYONE FOUND OUT?

ALL.
IT'S BALAGA!

BALAGA.
DRIVING MAD AT TWELVE MILES AN HOUR

ALL.
BALAGA!

BALAGA.
COMIN' STRAIGHT AT YOU
GET OUT MY WAY, GET OUT MY WAY

ALL.
BALAGA!

BALAGA.
DRINKING AND DANCING WITH MY RUSKA ROMA

ALL.
BALAGA!

BALAGA.
RIDING MY HORSES INTO THE GROUND
FOR MY FINE FINE GENTLEMEN
YESSIR HEY HO YESSIR
YESSIR YESSIR YESSIR

ALL.
MORE THAN ONCE!

BALAGA.
DRIVEN YOU ROUND WITH LADIES ON YOUR LAPS

ALL.
MORE THAN ONCE!

BALAGA.
TAKEN YOU PLACES NOT ON ANY MAPS

ALL.
MORE THAN ONCE!

BALAGA.
GALLOPED FASTER THAN ORDINARY MEN WOULD DARE

ALL.
MORE THAN ONCE!

BALAGA.
JUMPED MY TROIKA RIGHT INTO THE AIR!

AND I NEVER ASK FOR RUBLES
EXCEPT MAYBE ONCE A YEAR
I DON'T DO THIS FOR RUBLES
I DO IT CUZ I LIKE 'EM!

ALL.

AND WE LIKE BALAGA TOO!

ANATOLE.

WHOA...

ALL.

WHOA...

19. "THE ABDUCTION"

ANATOLE.
EVERYONE RAISE A GLASS! WHOA!

WELL, COMRADES
WE'VE HAD OUR FUN
LIVED, LAUGHED AND LOVED
FRIENDS OF MY YOUTH
WHEN SHALL WE MEET AGAIN?
I'M GOING ABROAD

GOODBYE MY GYPSY LOVERS
ALL MY REVELS HERE ARE OVER
WELL, GOODBYE, MATRYOSHA
KISS ME ONE LAST TIME, WHOA
REMEMBER ME TO STESHKA
THERE, GOODBYE, GOODBYE, GOODBYE
WISH ME LUCK MY GYPSY LOVERS
NOW GOODBYE, GOODBYE, GOODBYE

ALL.
GOODBYE MY GYPSY LOVERS
ALL MY REVELS HERE ARE OVER
WELL, GOODBYE, MATRYOSHA
KISS ME ONE LAST TIME, WHOA
REMEMBER ME TO STESHKA
THERE, GOODBYE, GOODBYE, GOODBYE
WISH ME LUCK MY GYPSY LOVERS
NOW GOODBYE, GOODBYE, GOODBYE

ANATOLE.
NOW DRINK!

ALL.
HURRAH!
SMASH THE GLASSES ON THE FLOOR!

(They dance.)

HEY! HEY! HEY! HEY!
HEY! HEY! HEY! HEY!

(They dance more. **PIERRE** *drunkenly raises a glass.)*

PIERRE.

> WHOA!
>
> HERE'S TO HAPPINESS, FREEDOM, AND LIFE!
> MAY YOUR TRAVELS BE SWIFT AS A SCYTHE CUTS THROUGH THE GRASS!
> MAY YOUR SORROWS BE COUNTED AND NUMBERED AS MANY
> AS DROPS OF WINE AND VODKA THAT STAY IN MY GLASS!
>
> *VSEGO HOROSHEGO*
> *NA POSOSHOK*
> *POEKHALI*
>
> *VSEGO HOROSHEGO*
> *NA POSOSHOK*
> *POEKHALI*

ALL.

> *VSEGO HOROSHEGO*
> *NA POSOSHOK*
> *POEKHALI*
>
> *VSEGO HOROSHEGO*
> *NA POSOSHOK*
> *POEKHALI*
> *NA POSOSHOK*
> *POEKHALI!*
>
> Come on, let's go!...
>
> > *(They start to leave.)*

ANATOLE.

> NO, WAIT!
> SHUT THE DOOR!
> FIRST WE HAVE TO SIT DOWN!
> THAT'S THE WAY
>
> IT'S A RUSSIAN CUSTOM
>
> > *(They shut the door and all sit down for a moment.)*
>
> ALL RIGHT
>
> > *(They start to leave.)*

DOLOKHOV.

> WAIT, WAIT, WAIT, WAIT!
> WHERE'S THE FUR CLOAK?
> I HAVE HEARD WHAT ELOPEMENTS ARE LIKE
> SHE'LL RUSH OUT MORE DEAD THAN ALIVE
> JUST IN THE THINGS SHE'S WEARING
> IF YOU DELAY AT ALL, THERE'LL BE TEARS AND "PAPA" AND "MAMA"
> AND SHE'S FROZEN IN A MINUTE AND MUST GO BACK
>
> BUT YOU WRAP THE FUR CLOAK ROUND HER
> AND YOU CARRY HER TO THE SLEIGH
> THAT'S THE WAY
> THAT'S THE WAY

ALL.

> THAT'S THE WAY
> THAT'S THE WAY

BALAGA.

> LET'S GET OUTTA HERE!
>
> AND THE TROIKA TORE DOWN NIKITSKI BOULEVARD
> WHOA! GIDDYUP, NOW! WHOA! WHOA!

ALL.

> HEY BALAGA
> HO BALAGA
> HEY HEY HO BALAGA
> HEY HEY BALAGA
> THE FAMOUS TROIKA DRIVER
>
> HEY BALAGA
> HO BALAGA
> HEY HEY HEY BALAGA
> HEY HEY BALAGA
> THE FAMOUS TROIKA DRIVER

DOLOKHOV.

> WHEN THEY REACHED THE GATE DOLOKHOV WHISTLED
> THE WHISTLE WAS ANSWERED, AND A MAIDSERVANT RAN OUT

MAIDSERVANT.

> COME IN THROUGH THE COURTYARD OR YOU'LL BE SEEN;
> SHE'LL COME OUT DIRECTLY

DOLOKHOV.
>DOLOKHOV STAYED BY THE GATE
>ANATOLE FOLLOWED THE MAID INTO THE COURTYARD
>TURNED THE CORNER, RAN UP TO THE PORCH

>>(**ANATOLE** *is stopped by* **MARYA D.**)

MARYA D.
>YOU WILL NOT ENTER MY HOUSE, SCOUNDREL!

DOLOKHOV.
>ANATOLE, COME BACK!
>BETRAYED! BETRAYED!
>BETRAYED, ANATOLE! BETRAYED!
>COME BACK!
>BETRAYED, ANATOLE! BETRAYED! BETRAYED!

>>(**DOLOKHOV** *rushes in and rescues* **ANATOLE**. *They flee.*)

PART V

Chapter 10

20. "IN MY HOUSE"

MARYA D.
>YOU SHAMELESS GOOD-FOR-NOTHING
>YOU VILE, SHAMELESS GIRL
>IN MY HOUSE
>IN MY HOUSE
>A NICE GIRL! VERY NICE!
>
>YOU DIRTY NASTY WENCH OF A THING
>NOW DON'T YOU SAY ONE WORD
>IN MY HOUSE
>IN MY HOUSE
>HORRID GIRL, HUSSY!
>
>IT'S LUCKY FOR HIM HE ESCAPED, BUT I'LL FIND HIM
>NOW YOU LISTEN TO ME WHEN I SPEAK TO YOU!
>NOW YOU LISTEN TO ME WHEN I SPEAK TO YOU!
>IN MY HOUSE!
>IN MY HOUSE!
>DO YOU HEAR WHAT I AM SAYING OR NOT?

SONYA.
>NATASHA'S WHOLE BODY SHOOK
>WITH NOISELESS, CONVULSIVE SOBS
>MARYA TOUCHED HER HAND TO HER FACE

NATASHA.
>DON'T TOUCH ME!
>LET ME BE! WHAT IS IT TO ME? I SHALL DIE!

MARYA D.

>WHAT ARE WE TO TELL YOUR FATHER EH?
>IN MY HOUSE!
>IN MY HOUSE!
>WHAT ARE WE TO TELL PRINCE ANDREY EH?
>OH WHAT DO WE TELL YOUR BETROTHED?

NATASHA.

>I HAVE NO BETROTHED, I HAVE REFUSED HIM!

SONYA.

>NATASHA, COME HERE, KISS ME
>PRESS YOUR WET FACE TO MINE

NATASHA.

>DON'T TOUCH ME!

MARYA D.

>WHY DIDN'T HE COME TO THE HOUSE?
>WHY DIDN'T HE OPENLY ASK FOR YOUR HAND?
>YOU WERE NOT KEPT UNDER LOCK AND KEY!
>CARRYING YOU OFF LIKE SOME GYPSY GIRL!
>AND IF HE HAD CARRIED YOU OFF, DON'T YOU THINK
>>YOUR FATHER WOULD HAVE FOUND HIM?
>YOUR FATHER, I KNOW HIM
>HE WILL CHALLENGE HIM TO A DUEL AND WHAT THEN,
>>WILL THAT BE ALL RIGHT EH?
>HE'S A SCOUNDREL, HE'S A WRETCH! THAT'S A FACT!

NATASHA.

>HE IS BETTER THAN ANY OF YOU I SAY
>HE IS BETTER THAN ANY OF YOU I SAY
>WHY DID YOU INTERFERE! OH GOD, WHAT IS IT ALL?!
>WHAT IS IT?!
>WHO ARE YOU TO TELL ME ANYTHING?!
>SONYA, WHY?!
>GO AWAY!
>EVERYONE, GO AWAY!
>
>MARYA DMITRYEVNA TRIED TO SPEAK AGAIN BUT
>>NATASHA CRIED OUT
>GO AWAY! GO AWAY! YOU ALL HATE AND DESPISE ME!
>AND SHE THREW HERSELF DOWN ON THE SOFA

MARYA D.
> NATASHA!
> NATALYA...
>
> I PUT A PILLOW UNDER HER HEAD
> COVERED HER WITH TWO QUILTS
> BROUGHT HER A GLASS OF LIME-FLOWER WATER
> BUT NATASHA DID NOT RESPOND
> WELL, LET HER SLEEP
> LET HER SLEEP

>> (**MARYA D.** *leaves.*)

NATASHA.
> BUT NATASHA WAS NOT ASLEEP
> HER FACE WAS PALE
> HER EYES WIDE OPEN
> ALL THAT NIGHT SHE DID NOT SLEEP OR WEEP
> SHE SAT AT THE WINDOW
> WAITING FOR HIM

21. "A CALL TO PIERRE"

*(A **SERVANT** hands a letter to **PIERRE**.)*

SERVANT.
> A LETTER FROM MARYA DMITRYEVNA ASKING YOU TO
>   COME AND VISIT HER
> ON A MATTER OF GREAT IMPORTANCE
> RELATING TO ANDREY BOLKONSKY AND HIS BETROTHED

PIERRE.
> WHAT?
> WHAT CAN THEY WANT WITH ME?

(He arrives at Marya D.'s.)

MARYA D.
> PIERRE, OLD FRIEND I'M SORRY IT'S LATE
> I'M SORRY I HAVEN'T SEEN YOU ABOUT
> WHERE HAVE YOU BEEN?
> WHERE HAVE YOU BEEN?

PIERRE.
> I HAVE BEEN STUDYING

MARYA D.
> PIERRE OLD FRIEND WE NEED YOUR HELP
> PIERRE OLD FRIEND THE FAMILY NAME
> WE NEED YOUR HELP
> WE NEED YOUR HELP
> THERE'S RUIN AT THE DOOR

PIERRE.
> MARYA?

MARYA D.
> NATASHA HAS LET DOWN THE FAMILY

PIERRE.
> WHAT?

MARYA D.
> NATASHA HAS BROKEN WITH ANDREY

PIERRE.
> WHAT?

MARYA D.
> NATASHA HAS TRIED TO ELOPE

PIERRE.
>WHAT?

MARYA D.
>NATASHA AND ANATOLE KURAGIN!

PIERRE.
>WHAT?

MARYA D.
>WE NEED YOUR HELP
>WE NEED YOUR HELP
>THERE'S RUIN AT THE DOOR

PIERRE.
>NATASHA, THAT CHARMING GIRL?
>I CAN'T BELIEVE MY EARS
>SO I AM NOT THE ONLY MAN
>CHAINED TO A BAD WOMAN
>AND ANATOLE, THAT STUPID CHILD
>THEY'LL LOCK HIM UP FOR YEARS
>FOR ANATOLE IS A MARRIED MAN!

MARYA D.
>MARRIED? HE'S MARRIED?

PIERRE.
>YES

MARYA D.
>OH WAIT 'TIL I TELL HER

PIERRE.
>POOR ANDREY

MARYA D.
>AND WHEN ANDREY COMES HOME
>HE WILL CHALLENGE ANATOLE TO A DUEL
>AND GET HIMSELF KILLED
>AND ALL WILL BE RUINED
>
>YOU MUST GO SEE YOUR BROTHER-IN-LAW
>AND TELL HIM THAT HE MUST LEAVE MOSCOW
>AND NOT DARE TO LET ME SET MY EYES ON HIM AGAIN

PIERRE.
>AT ONCE

Chapter 11

22. "FIND ANATOLE"

PIERRE.
>ANATOLE, FIND ANATOLE
>ANATOLE, FIND ANATOLE
>THE BLOOD RUSHES TO MY HEART
>IT'S DIFFICULT TO BREATHE
>ANATOLE, FIND ANATOLE
>ANATOLE, FIND ANATOLE
>NOT AT THE ICE HILLS
>NOT AT MATRESHKA'S
>NOT AT KOMONENO'S
>ANATOLE, FIND ANATOLE
>ANATOLE, FIND ANATOLE
>TO THE CLUB
>
>AND AT THE CLUB ALL IS GOING ON AS USUAL
>THE MEMBERS EAT THEIR DINNERS
>AND GOSSIP IN SMALL GROUPS

PIERRE & CHORUS.
>HAVE I HEARD OF KURAGIN'S ABDUCTION?
>IS IT TRUE NATASHA IS RUINED?

PIERRE.
>NONSENSE, NONSENSE
>NOTHING HAS HAPPENED
>EVERYTHING IS FINE
>
>*(Pierre's house.)*

ANATOLE.
>NATASHA
>NATASHA
>IT IS ESSENTIAL THAT I SEE NATASHA
>HOW CAN I SEE HER?

HÉLÈNE.
>ANATOLE, COME ANATOLE
>ANATOLE, HUSH ANATOLE

(Marya D.'s house.)

NATASHA.
> WHAT? WHAT?
> I DON'T BELIEVE THAT HE IS MARRIED
> I DON'T BELIEVE YOU
> AND I STARE LIKE A HUNTED WOUNDED ANIMAL
> HE CAN'T BE MARRIED!

(Pierre's house.)

SERVANT. *(To* **PIERRE.***)*
> GOOD EVENING SIR
> PRINCE ANATOLE IS IN THE DRAWING ROOM WITH THE COUNTESS

HÉLÈNE.
> AH, PIERRE
> SWEET HUSBAND
> YOU DON'T KNOW WHAT A PLIGHT OUR ANATOLE HAS HAD

PIERRE.
> BE QUIET
> I WILL NOT GREET YOU
> AT THIS MOMENT YOU ARE MORE REPULSIVE TO ME THAN EVER
>
> ANATOLE, COME ANATOLE
> ANATOLE, MUST SPEAK TO YOU

ANATOLE.
> ANATOLE FOLLOWED WITH HIS USUAL JAUNTY STEP
> BUT HIS FACE BETRAYED ANXIETY

PIERRE.
> PIERRE CLOSED THE DOOR AND ADDRESSED ANATOLE WITHOUT LOOKING AT HIM

23. "PIERRE & ANATOLE"

*(During this scene, **NATASHA** prepares to poison herself.)*

PIERRE.
> YOU PROMISED COUNTESS ROSTOVA TO MARRY HER AND WERE ABOUT TO ELOPE, IS THAT SO?

ANATOLE.
> *MON CHER*
> I DON'T CONSIDER MYSELF BOUND TO ANSWER QUESTIONS PUT TO ME IN THAT TONE

PIERRE.
> MY FACE, ALREADY PALE
> BECOMES DISTORTED BY FURY
> I SEIZE YOU BY THE COLLAR WITH MY BIG BIG HANDS
> AND I SHAKE YOU FROM SIDE TO SIDE
> UNTIL YOUR FACE SHOWS A SUFFICIENT DEGREE OF TERROR
> WHEN I TELL YOU I MUST TALK TO YOU!

ANATOLE.
> COME NOW, THIS IS STUPID!
> WHAT WHAT DON'T DON'T!

PIERRE.
> YOU'RE A SCOUNDREL AND A BLACKGUARD
> AND I DON'T KNOW WHAT DEPRIVES ME OF THE PLEASURE
> OF SMASHING YOUR HEAD IN WITH THIS!
>
> *(He takes a heavy paperweight and lifts it threateningly, but at once puts it back in its place.)*
>
> DID YOU PROMISE TO MARRY HER?

ANATOLE.
> I DIDN'T THINK OF IT
> I NEVER PROMISED, BECAUSE –

PIERRE.
> HAVE YOU ANY LETTERS OF HERS?

ANY LETTERS?

I SHAN'T BE VIOLENT, DON'T BE AFRAID

    (**ANATOLE** *hands* **PIERRE** *a pack of letters.*)

FIRST, THE LETTERS
SECOND, TOMORROW YOU MUST GET OUT OF MOSCOW

ANATOLE.

    BUT HOW CAN I?

PIERRE.

    THIRD
    YOU MUST NEVER BREATHE A WORD OF WHAT HAS
        HAPPENED BETWEEN YOU AND THE COUNTESS
    NOW I KNOW I CAN'T PREVENT YOUR DOING SO
    BUT IF YOU HAVE A SPARK OF CONSCIENCE –

    PIERRE PACES THE ROOM SEVERAL TIMES IN SILENCE

ANATOLE.

    ANATOLE SITS AT A TABLE FROWNING AND BITING HIS
        LIPS

PIERRE.

    AFTER ALL, YOU MUST UNDERSTAND
    THAT BESIDES YOUR PLEASURE
    THERE IS SUCH A THING AS OTHER PEOPLE, AND THEIR
        HAPPINESS AND PEACE
    AND THAT YOU ARE RUINING A WHOLE LIFE
    FOR THE SAKE OF AMUSING YOURSELF!
    AMUSE YOURSELF WITH WOMEN LIKE MY WIFE
    WITH THEM YOU'RE WITHIN YOUR RIGHTS
    BUT TO PROMISE A YOUNG GIRL TO MARRY HER
    TO DECEIVE, TO KIDNAP
    DON'T YOU UNDERSTAND THAT THAT'S AS CRUEL
    AS BEATING AN OLD MAN OR A CHILD?

ANATOLE.

    WELL I DON'T KNOW ABOUT THAT, EH?
    I DON'T KNOW THAT AND I DON'T WANT TO
    BUT YOU HAVE USED SUCH WORDS TO ME
    "SCOUNDREL" AND SO ON
    WHICH AS A MAN OF HONOR

PIERRE.
>I WILL NOT ALLOW ANYONE TO USE

PIERRE.
>IS IT SATISFACTION YOU WANT?

ANATOLE.
>YOU COULD AT LEAST TAKE BACK YOUR WORDS, EH?
>IF YOU WANT ME TO DO AS YOU WISH

>>(**NATASHA** *drinks the poison.*)

PIERRE.
>FINE I TAKE THEM BACK, I TAKE THEM BACK!
>AND I ASK YOU TO FORGIVE ME
>AND IF YOU REQUIRE MONEY FOR YOUR JOURNEY –

ANATOLE.
>ANATOLE SMILED
>THE REFLECTION OF THAT BASE AND CRINGING SMILE
>WHICH PIERRE KNEW SO WELL IN HIS WIFE
>REVOLTED HIM

PIERRE.
>OH, VILE AND HEARTLESS BROOD!

ANATOLE.
>NEXT DAY ANATOLE LEFT
>FOR PETERSBURG!

Chapter 12

24. "NATASHA VERY ILL"

SONYA.
>NATASHA VERY ILL
>THE WHOLE HOUSE
>A STATE OF ALARM AND COMMOTION
>NATASHA VERY ILL
>HAVING POISONED HERSELF
>WITH A BIT OF ARSENIC
>SHE WOKE ME IN THE MIDDLE OF THE NIGHT
>AND TOLD ME WHAT SHE HAD DONE
>AND THE DOCTORS
>AND THE ANTIDOTES
>AND NOW SHE IS OUT OF DANGER
>BUT STILL SO WEAK
>AND ANDREY IS TO RETURN
>WE WAIT WITH DREAD

25. "PIERRE & ANDREY"

(**ANDREY** *visits* **PIERRE**.)

ANDREY.
WELL, HOW ARE YOU?
STILL GETTING STOUTER?

PIERRE.
THERE'S A NEW WRINKLE
ON YOUR FOREHEAD OLD FRIEND

ANDREY.
IT'S GOOD TO SEE YOU
I'VE BEEN AWAY TOO LONG

PIERRE.
MY FRIEND, YOU ARE IN NEED
YOUR FACE IS GLOOMY

ANDREY.
NO, I AM WELL
THERE'S A WAR GOING ON

FORGIVE ME FOR TROUBLING YOU
I HAVE RECEIVED A REFUSAL FROM COUNTESS ROSTOVA
AND HAVE HEARD REPORTS OF YOUR BROTHER-IN-LAW
   HAVING SOUGHT HER HAND
OR SOMETHING OF THAT KIND
IS THIS TRUE?

PIERRE.
SOMETHING OF THAT KIND

ANDREY.
HERE ARE HER LETTERS
PLEASE GIVE THEM TO THE COUNTESS

PIERRE.
NATASHA IS ILL
SHE HAS BEEN AT DEATH'S DOOR

ANDREY.
I MUCH REGRET HER ILLNESS

PIERRE.
AND HE SMILED LIKE HIS FATHER

COLDLY, MALICIOUSLY
ANDREY.
WELL, IT DOESN'T MATTER
PIERRE.
YOU TOLD ME ONCE
A FALLEN WOMAN SHOULD BE FORGIVEN
ANDREY.
BUT I DIDN'T SAY THAT I COULD FORGIVE
I CAN'T

YES, ASK HER HAND AGAIN
BE MAGNANIMOUS, AND SO ON
YES, THAT WOULD BE VERY NOBLE
BUT I CAN'T BE THAT MAN
IF YOU WISH TO BE MY FRIEND
NEVER SPEAK OF THAT AGAIN

WELL, GOODBYE

*(**PIERRE** takes the letters to **NATASHA**.)*

Chapter 13

26. "PIERRE & NATASHA"

PIERRE.
>NATASHA WAS STANDING
>IN THE MIDDLE OF THE DRAWING ROOM
>WITH A PALE YET STEADY FACE
>WHEN I APPEARED IN THE DOORWAY
>SHE GREW FLUSTERED AND I HURRIED TO HER
>I THOUGHT THAT SHE WOULD GIVE ME HER HAND
>BUT INSTEAD SHE STOPPED
>BREATHING HEAVILY
>HER THIN ARMS HANGING LIFELESSLY
>JUST IN THE VERY POSE
>SHE USED TO STAND IN AS A YOUNG GIRL
>WHEN SHE WENT TO THE MIDDLE OF THE BALLROOM TO SING
>BUT THE LOOK ON HER FACE WAS QUITE DIFFERENT

NATASHA.
>PETER KIRILOVICH –

PIERRE.
>PIERRE

NATASHA.
>PRINCE BOLKONSKY WAS YOUR FRIEND –
>HE IS YOUR FRIEND
>HE ONCE TOLD ME THAT I SHOULD TURN TO YOU

PIERRE.
>PIERRE SNIFFED AS HE LOOKED AT HER, BUT HE DIDN'T SPEAK
>'TIL THEN HE HAD REPROACHED HER, AND TRIED TO DESPISE HER
>BUT NOW HE FELT SUCH PITY FOR HER
>THAT THERE WAS NO ROOM IN HIS SOUL FOR REPROACH

NATASHA.
>HE IS HERE NOW

TELL HIM TO –
TELL HIM TO FORGIVE ME

PIERRE.
YES, I WILL TELL HIM TO FORGIVE YOU
BUT, HE GAVE ME YOUR LETTERS –

NATASHA.
NO, I KNOW THAT ALL IS OVER
I KNOW THAT IT NEVER CAN BE
BUT STILL I'M TORMENTED BY THE WRONGS I'VE DONE HIM
TELL HIM THAT I BEG HIM TO FORGIVE, FORGIVE
FORGIVE ME FOR EVERYTHING

PIERRE.
YES I WILL TELL HIM, TELL HIM EVERYTHING
BUT –
BUT I SHOULD LIKE TO KNOW ONE THING
DID YOU LOVE
DID YOU LOVE THAT BAD MAN?

NATASHA.
DON'T CALL HIM BAD
BUT I DON'T KNOW, I DON'T KNOW AT ALL

PIERRE.
SHE BEGAN TO CRY
AND A GREATER SENSE OF PITY, TENDERNESS, AND LOVE OVERFLOWED PIERRE'S HEART
HE FELT THE TEARS BEGIN TO TRICKLE UNDERNEATH HIS SPECTACLES
AND HE HOPED THAT NO ONE WOULD SEE

WE WON'T SPEAK OF IT ANYMORE
WE WON'T SPEAK OF IT, MY DEAR
BUT ONE THING I BEG OF YOU, CONSIDER ME YOUR FRIEND
AND IF YOU EVER NEED HELP, OR SIMPLY TO OPEN YOUR HEART TO SOMEONE
NOT NOW, BUT WHEN YOUR MIND IS CLEAR
THINK OF ME –

PIERRE GREW CONFUSED

NATASHA.
>DON'T SPEAK TO ME LIKE THAT
>I AM NOT WORTH IT

PIERRE.
>STOP, STOP, STOP!
>YOU HAVE YOUR WHOLE LIFE BEFORE YOU –

NATASHA.
>BEFORE ME? NO, ALL IS OVER FOR ME!

PIERRE.
>ALL OVER?
>
>>*(Music stops.)*
>
>If I were not myself,
>but the brightest, handsomest,
>best man on earth,
>and if I were free –
>I would get down on my knees this minute
>and ask you for your hand
>and for your love.
>
>>*(Music resumes.)*

NATASHA.
>AND FOR THE FIRST TIME IN MANY DAYS
>I WEEP TEARS OF GRATITUDE
>TEARS OF TENDERNESS
>TEARS OF THANKS
>AND GLANCING AT PIERRE
>OH PIERRE
>I LEAVE THE ROOM SMILING

PIERRE.
>AND RESTRAINING TEARS OF TENDERNESS
>TEARS OF JOY WHICH CHOKE ME
>I THROW MY FUR COAT ON MY SHOULDERS
>UNABLE TO FIND THE SLEEVES
>
>OUTSIDE, MY GREAT BROAD CHEST
>BREATHES IN DEEP THE AIR WITH JOY
>DESPITE THE TEN DEGREES OF FROST
>AND I GET INTO MY SLEIGH

27. "THE GREAT COMET OF 1812"

PIERRE.
>WHERE TO NOW?
>WHERE CAN I GO NOW?
>NOT TO THE CLUB
>NOT TO PAY CALLS
>
>MANKIND SEEMS SO PITIFUL
>SO POOR
>COMPARED TO THAT SOFTENED, GRATEFUL LAST GLANCE
>SHE GAVE ME THROUGH HER TEARS

CHORUS.
>IT WAS CLEAR AND COLD
>ABOVE THE DIRTY STREETS
>ABOVE THE BLACK ROOFS
>STRETCHED THE DARK STARRY SKY

PIERRE.
>THIS VAST FIRMAMENT
>OPEN TO MY EYES
>WET WITH TEARS

CHORUS.
>AND THERE IN THE MIDDLE
>ABOVE PRECHISTENSKY BOULEVARD
>SURROUNDED AND SPRINKLED ON ALL SIDES BY STARS
>SHINES THE GREAT COMET OF 1812
>THE BRILLIANT COMET OF 1812

PIERRE.
>THE COMET SAID TO PORTEND
>UNTOLD HORRORS
>AND THE END OF THE WORLD
>
>BUT FOR ME
>THE COMET BRINGS NO FEAR
>NO, I GAZE JOYFULLY
>
>AND THIS BRIGHT STAR
>HAVING TRACED ITS PARABOLA
>WITH INEXPRESSIBLE SPEED
>THROUGH IMMEASURABLE SPACE

SEEMS SUDDENLY
TO HAVE STOPPED
LIKE AN ARROW PIERCING THE EARTH
STOPPED FOR ME

IT SEEMS TO ME
THAT THIS COMET
FEELS ME
FEELS MY SOFTENED AND UPLIFTED SOUL
AND MY NEWLY MELTED HEART
NOW BLOSSOMING
INTO A NEW LIFE